RESISTING LILY

THE KINCAID SERIES

BOOK 2

BJ Wane

Copyright © 2023 by BJ Wane
All rights reserved.

This book or any portion thereof may not be reproduced or used in any manner whatsoever without the express written permission of the author except for the use of brief quotations in a book review.

Editors:
Kate Richards & Nanette Sipes

Cover Design & Formatting:
Joe Dugdale (sylv.net)

PUBLISHED BY BLUE DAHLIA

DISCLAIMER

This contemporary romantic suspense contains adult themes such as power exchange and sexual scenes. Please do not read if these offend you.

DEDICATION

This book is dedicated to my awesome editors, Kate Richardson and Nanette Sipes, and my wonderful beta readers, Sandie Buckley, Gaynor Jones, and Kathy Heare Watts. Thank you so much, ladies – I couldn't do it without you!

CONTENTS

Chapter One	7
Chapter Two	31
Chapter Three	59
Chapter Four	82
Chapter Five	106
Chapter Six	130
Chapter Seven	155
Chapter Eight	176
Chapter Nine	198
Chapter Ten	219
Chapter Eleven	241
Chapter Twelve	263
Chapter Thirteen	286
About BJ Wane	299
More Books by BJ Wane	301
Contact BJ Wane	303

Chapter One

"Shit."

With an annoyed downward thrust, Reed Kincaid jabbed the pitchfork into the hay bale and pulled his vibrating cell phone out of his pocket. As he thought, the text was from his highway patrol partner, John Wainscott, the fourth today. Disregarding it the same as the others, he tucked the phone back in his pocket.

"Ignoring a problem doesn't make it go away."

Reed glared at his younger brother, Slade, from across the stacks of hay. "You ought to know."

Slade cocked his head, a bead of sweat rolling down his neck. "I deal with my issues in my own way, my own time. You're avoiding yours altogether."

They were working in the large storage barn today, loading fresh straw for the horse stalls and feed to transport to the stable and barn. Slade grabbed the embedded hay bale D-hooks and tossed the bundled fodder onto the tractor bed, leaving Reed to scowl at his back.

"It's Saturday, and we're not on the clock today. John should sign the fucking papers and let his wife go. It's the least he can do considering his behavior during the two years before she had the good sense to call it quits."

Turning, Slade leaned his arms on the tractor hood and regarded him with a curl of his lips, his Stetson shielding his gray eyes. "You were John's best man at their wedding, and yet you never mention his wife by name."

Using the end of his T-shirt, Reed wiped the trickle of perspiration rolling down the side of his face, his muscles tensing from frustration at having another unwanted fact pointed out to him. "What's your point?" he asked with an edge to his tone. He sighed, bemoaning how quick he was to go on the defensive over anything alluding to his partner's wife, Lily Wainscott, when most times he was the mild-mannered, easygoing one between him, Slade, and their older brother, Brett.

"I'll leave you to figure that out for yourself." Slade swung up onto the tractor seat and started the engine. Shouting over the noise, he jerked a thumb toward the wide-open barn doors. "Meet me in the stable."

Reed nodded and lifted his hat to scrape his hair off his damp forehead before lowering his arm. He'd let it grow longer than usual, and his boss had already issued two warnings, reminders he was in violation of their codes. At one time, that would never have happened. Somehow, within the last year, he had quit caring so much about his career, his desire to join Slade daily in running the thirty-thousand-acre ranch he and his brothers inherited from their father overriding his enjoyment of working in law enforcement.

Following the tractor out of the barn, Reed lowered the brim of his Stetson against the bright afternoon sun. He welcomed the late-August heat seeping into his sore muscles while looking forward to the cooler fall temperatures. This year, there was Brett and Allie's summer wedding to look forward to during winter's long, tedious frigid days of less outdoor activity. Big brother had surprised everyone with his quick proposal to the woman he had spent so much effort trying to convince himself was not his type. Good thing Allie was one of those people who refused to take no for an answer when she wanted something, or someone, and knew when to pause when necessary. It was she who had insisted they wait almost a year before marrying, since Brett's divorce had just been finalized.

His partner, John, was the same, but not in a good way, like Allie. His future sister-in-law knew where to draw the line in her efforts to get what she wanted, and when to give up and walk away. John refused to grant his wife the divorce she filed for eight months ago after Reed had warned him repeatedly his cheating would cost him everything. When it did, the reality of losing her sent him into a tailspin of depression and anger that he continued to unload on Reed.

And he was fucking tired of John crying to him over losing Lily and swearing he couldn't live without her, claiming she was his one and only after spending the last three years involved in one affair after another. Lily, with her compassionate heart and hidden depths reflected in her golden-brown eyes any sane man would give his left nut to explore, deserved better. But John had refused to heed his advice then as now whenever Reed told him to stop dragging her to court to stall the divorce.

Yeah, Reed thought, striding toward the stables, John was a problem he intended to ignore on his day off. It was either that or go over to his house and knock some sense into the idiot. As much satisfaction as he would derive from planting his fist in his friend's lying, cheating face, Lily's disapproval stayed his hand. When he'd last seen John's wife, she'd been gazing at her estranged husband with sympathy and concern, telling Reed that John needed him more than ever, and asked him to please not abandon him.

Until that moment, he'd believed there wasn't anything Lily Wainscott could ask of him that he would deny her, but, God help him, he wanted to ditch his six-year friendship and partnership in the worst way.

Reed entered the stable, shoving aside thoughts about John and Lily. Hard work was a great antidote to plaguing issues, and when that wasn't enough by end of the day, he could always call a member of their exclusive group to join him tonight at Casey's. The nightclub he and his brothers had opened a few years ago had proved a profitable sideline, and with the upper floor renovated to hold private BDSM themed parties with friends in the lifestyle, it was the perfect escape to unwind and relieve stress.

They labored in companionable silence while unloading the tractor, but no matter how much sweat he worked up, Reed's thoughts still strayed to the one woman who was off-limits. He was proud of the way he'd kept his surprise masked when John first introduced him to Lily, considering the jolt of recognition seeing her again had given him. There had been two feet of snow on the ground when he had been in Casper testifying in a court case a year after hiring on with Wyoming Highway Patrol. Dealing with people who held no regard for others, like the perp fighting the DUI he had given him, always left him in a sour mood. That day, catching sight of Lily's selfless act of kindness to a homeless woman as he'd driven by a city park had reminded him there were still good people around.

Reed didn't need the truck's heater cranked on high when he slid behind the wheel. Having to make this trip into Casper to testify against a drunk driver fighting the loss of his license had left him hot enough under the collar to ward off the frigid cold. He slammed the truck door and tried to forget about the callous young man who insisted he'd done nothing wrong by driving while intoxicated. Too bad for him Reed's recollection of the guy's weaving in and out of traffic along the US highway between Casper and Cheyenne was excellent.

Dealing with such cold, self-centered individuals with no regard for others reminded him of why he'd left the Denver police department and returned home to Wyoming. At least as a highway patrol officer, he wasn't subjected daily to the worst of humankind. His tires crunched over the packed-down snow as he left the courthouse parking lot then turned the corner, intending to grab something for lunch before returning to work. Up ahead, an SUV pulled to the curb, a woman with long sable hair hopping out and grabbing his attention as she dashed over to a huddled figure sitting on the park bench.

She wrapped an arm around the older woman who appeared frail, and possibly homeless given her scanty attire and the beat-up bag at her feet. His curiosity piqued, he waited as they spoke in case this was a touchy family situation, wishing he could see more of the younger woman's face than her profile. He was about to offer assistance when it became obvious the older woman didn't want to leave her perch, but she finally complied, accepting whatever help the other woman was offering.

Her Good Samaritan ushered her across the street and into the hotel. The most the decades-old, run-down establishment offered now was cheap but clean rooms and creaky pipes in the bathrooms. He got a good look at the younger woman as she emerged alone from the hotel several minutes later, her face reflecting sadness but relief, and he assumed she had talked the homeless elder into staying. His interest kicked up another notch, this time in appreciation for both the kind act and an attractive, appealing woman.

As soon as she drove away, he got out and went inside the hotel to ensure the proprietor did right by both females.

Slade's cursing pulled Reed back to the present, and he put more effort into working. The memory of that hotel manager's face blanching when he showed him his badge still amused Reed. The man quickly turned, more willing to reveal Lily's name and how she and other volunteers from the local homeless shelter kept an eye on the "crazy old Asian lady" and would try to get her out of the frigid cold as much as possible since she refused to stay at the shelter. He only had Lily's first name, or he wouldn't have been so surprised when John first introduced him to his fiancée.

Reed retained a few other fond moments shared with Lily from getting to know her through John these last three years, but it was in his best interest to ignore them until he could let them and her go without regrets. Otherwise, he would remain in an emotional limbo, coping with feelings he should never have possessed for a friend's wife.

****

"You're quiet tonight."

Reed shrugged, avoiding eye contact with Jordon Myers, a good friend they had hired to manage Casey's. "I have a lot on my mind right now." He sipped his beer, swiveling on the barstool to scan the Saturday night crowd at Casey's. The music wasn't so loud people couldn't converse without yelling, but the boisterous enthusiasm coming from the group gathered around the mechanical bull reached across the ten thousand square foot space they'd spent months renovating. His mood lightened watching Allie mount the gyrating vault. "She's managed to master that thing in no time, hasn't she?"

Jordan nodded, grinning. "The more people bet against her, the more determined she's become. It's been fun to watch."

What's been even more entertaining to witness was Brett's slow downfall from bachelorhood. At forty and still battling a bitter divorce, his older brother by a year had sworn he wouldn't marry again, let alone get involved with a woman so much younger and opposite from his usual type. Allie had set her sights on Brett her first visit to Casey's at the start of summer, but it had taken a threat to her life before Brett caved to her wiles. It still surprised Reed and Slade how quick Brett had been to propose after coming close to losing her.

"Speaking of watching..." Reed jerked a thumb toward Brett who stood with arms crossed and booted feet planted apart, his focus on Allie's swaying body.

"Who'd have thought?" Jordan lifted a finger to the two women who settled on barstools at the other end. "Gotta earn my pay. Are you joining the get-together upstairs after closing?"

"Plan to, after I help you straighten up down here." He and his brothers were raised not to shirk their duties regardless of the wealth that enabled them to hire others to do the work. Their father might have been a poor husband and somewhat lackadaisical parent, leaving a lot of their summer supervision when they were at the ranch up to his foreman, but he took the time to instill a good work ethic in his three sons.

"Catch you later, then."

Jordan strolled down to the women who kept casting flirtatious glances their way, but Reed found himself disinterested, and Jordan wouldn't play the game as long as he was with Bianca. Left alone,

Reed wished Slade had come out with him instead of waiting until they got together upstairs after closing. He and Brett were used to their youngest brother preferring solitude to socializing ever since he ended his days as a military sniper. If that's how he needed to cope with his demons, he had their support. That didn't keep them from giving Slade a hard time about it though.

Reed took another drink before turning to scope out the crowd, looking for a table of friends he could join rather than someone new to strike up a conversation with. His gaze landed on the mechanical bull corner as Brett reached down to assist Allie up from the floor. She must have lost her latest battle to beat her record, but that didn't keep her from laughing at herself as his brother hauled her against him. The look of indulgence and profound caring reflected on Brett's face so often when he was with her still took some getting used to. While happy for Brett's good fortune, the tight clutch gripping Reed's abdomen again proved what he wouldn't admit aloud – how much he had been itching for such a relationship with one person lately.

Swearing under his breath, he forced himself to focus on Brett and Allie heading toward him instead of Lily's concerned, sad eyes the last time he'd been in the same room with John, listening to him plead with her for another chance then go off on her when she shook her head. In the eight months since she left him and filed for divorce, John had subjected Reed to bitter tirades and bouts of drunken weeping regrets over and over, getting angry with him when he refused to get involved or told him to own up to his wrongdoings and let her go. Reed had lost count of how many times he'd told himself he didn't care what either of them did with their marriage as long as they left him out of it.

Lying to himself was much easier than facing the truth.

"Maybe you should have stayed home with Slade tonight," Brett said, taking the stool next to Reed and wrapping an arm around Allie's waist to assist her to perch on his thigh.

Allie leaned forward and placed a hand on Reed's knee, the rings adorning each finger glinting under the pendant bar light, her blonde head tilted. "Bad day, Reed?"

Reed schooled his expression to mask his lingering annoyance with John's persistent calls, berating himself for letting his partner's issues affect Reed's day off. No wonder he was taking a hard look at resigning from law enforcement altogether.

"A persistent aggravation is all. I'm fine."

Brett cocked his head, and Reed bristled at his probing stare. "As in your partner, John? And, don't bite my head off for asking."

Reed blew out a breath and relaxed his tense shoulders. Since they were kids, he'd been the one to soothe ruffled feathers or offer an ear. Not so much lately, though, always on edge after spending eight hours cooped up in his department cruiser listening to John cursing and weeping over Lily. He used to love patrolling the Wyoming highways with his friend and partner. Not anymore. "Yes, the same old crap, I assume. I haven't answered his calls today." His phone buzzed, and he pulled it out, rolling his eyes before he noticed his captain's number on the display screen.

Wondering at a call from his boss interrupting his day off, he held up the phone to his brother, saying, "I'm going to take this outside." Reed brought the phone to his ear and slid off the stool to head for the front door. "Hey, Captain, what's up?"

"Can you get someplace quiet, Kincaid?" Captain Carmichael asked as Reed grabbed the door handle.

"Doing so now, sir." Growing suspicious with a ball of dread forming in his gut, Reed stepped outside and moved away from the doorway before speaking again. "Sorry. I'm at Casey's but outside now." A tangible hesitation on the other end, very unlike his straightforward, blunt-speaking superior, caused his stomach to cramp. "Captain?"

"I'm sorry, Reed. John's dead, apparent suicide or accidental overdose. We'll have to wait on the coroner's report."

Captain Carmichael's statement hit Reed with a shock wave of disbelief followed by a body-jarring stab of grief. His first thought was instant denial – there was no way John would take his own life or overdose. For one thing, his partner was too self-centered to even consider going that way, and he would never abuse his body with drugs. He thought too highly of his physique and worked daily to stay in shape.

"Who found him?" Reed asked, a wave of guilt slithering through him.

Here he'd spent the day cursing John for trying to intrude on his time off by pestering him with his problems and, instead, his friend and partner had been drowning in desperation. God help him, did he turn his back on John when he'd needed him most?

"His brother, Jason. Called headquarters when he couldn't get hold of him and he didn't answer the door even though his vehicle was in the drive. He swears there is no way John overdosed, not even by accident. I'm inclined to agree."

"Which leaves suicide? I'm not going there, not without proof. He wouldn't go that way, Captain." *Or did I miss the signs because of Lily?* God, he hoped he didn't have to live with that on his conscience.

"I'm calling it an accidental death until I get the autopsy report," Michaels returned in the firm tone Reed knew better than to argue with.

They spoke another minute then he ended the call, trying to digest that mind-numbing news. With leaden footsteps, he walked around the side of Casey's and sank down on the steps leading to the upper floor, memories assailing him, the good and bad times of the six years he'd known John. The two of them had hung out together a lot after becoming partners, Reed welcoming John's friendship and company coming on the heels of his permanent return to Wyoming. With Brett still practicing corporate law at a big firm in San Antonio and Slade exhausting himself working the ranch from sunup to sundown, Reed had spent the majority of his days off with John until he met Lily. It didn't take long after that for their relationship to sour.

Lily.

Thinking of the woman Reed was halfway in love with and wondering how she was taking the news of her husband's death left him even more shaken.

****

Reed parked on the tree-lined residential street several doors down from the house John and Lily had lived in together before she'd left and filed for divorce eight months ago. He sat a moment, wondering how she felt being back in the cottage-style home she had taken great pains to decorate and make their own. The few times they had invited him for dinner, she'd shown him the most recent changes she'd made, inside and out, her face suffused with unmistakable pride and pleasure. Eyeing the people gathered out front and watching others come and go from inside, he would bet she had dreaded joining John's colleagues and friends in saying their final goodbyes today in the home she had shared both good and bad times with her husband. Maybe as much as he did, although, that was difficult to imagine given his reluctance to get out of his vehicle and the remorse still plaguing him.

Forcing himself to do the necessary and right thing, Reed stepped onto the sidewalk, shut the door, and inhaled the fresh scent of recently mowed grass.

One more week until September, his favorite time of year, something he and Lily shared in common. There were other things he'd come to discover since John introduced them four years ago, but he firmly closed the lid on going through a mental tally of them. The next hour of fulfilling his obligation to his late partner and the department and coming face-to-face with Lily's grief would be hard enough to get through.

Reed strode up the walkway to the front door, pausing to clasp the outstretched hand of fellow officer, James Deitrich.

"I'm sorry, Kincaid. It's rough, losing a partner under any circumstances. How are you doing?"

He could feel the sympathetic gazes of the few others congregated outside and stiffened against their pity. "About as well as you and everyone else here, I imagine. I rode with him every day and never noticed he was headed toward this end. I regret that more than anything."

The autopsy report had been inconclusive, leaving the cause of death at accidental. Reed suspected that might have been so Lily could inherit John's life insurance that likely contained a suicide exemption.

"Given his actions, none of us thought John

would take a divorce so hard."

Reed nodded in agreement along with the others. He was the only one privy to his partner's constant meltdowns these past eight months, ever since Lily had finally left him over his numerous infidelities. In his opinion, she had waited two years and ten months too long, considering her husband first cheated on her two months after they were married. Reed had been in the dark about their marital strife that first year and wished he could have stayed oblivious to Lily's suffering. Instead, his friendship and partnership had slowly deteriorated to the point he had filled out his resignation the night before John died, intending to turn it in the following Monday morning. Tomorrow, a week later than planned, was soon enough, and at least he'd spared John learning his actions had also driven off his best friend and partner, not that Reed believed John would ever have changed his ways.

"I'd best pay my respects to his wife. Thanks, guys." Reed lifted a hand as he opened the door with the other, grateful he was retiring from law enforcement with all his other friendships still intact.

Bracing for the impact of seeing Lily again, he entered the house and paused to search the crowd of mourners, wanting this over with as soon as possible. He found her standing by a food-laden table, recognizing her from the back by the waist-length cascade of rich mahogany hair. Not too many women wore their hair that long by the time they were thirty-one, and, more often than not, she wore it in a thick braid. John had preferred her to wear it loose, a concession she had stopped granting him when he started fighting the divorce. Until today.

Lily turned to face the next person to come up to her, black-pleated skirt swishing around her knees. Reed's gut clenched at seeing the strain on her pale face, the same painful sucker punch he'd experienced when John introduced them. He sucked in a breath, as deep as possible with the lump lodged in his throat, and strove to get his emotions in check before approaching his partner's grieving widow. Maybe, if he kept thinking of her in those terms, he could refrain from making the mistake of exposing the craving her nearness always stirred to life. He'd spent too much time and effort keeping his attraction to John's wife under wraps to reveal anything now, and intended to continue doing so until he got over it.

Reed moved her way, reaching her side the moment Lily turned those whiskey, regret-filled eyes toward him, her gaze filling with unshed tears.

"Reed, why did he do this? I could almost believe one of his women was responsible better than this," she whispered in a tremulous voice.

Lily leaned in to him, and he saw no way out of embracing her, insisting his loose hold was an offer of comfort, nothing else. He'd gotten good at lying to himself these past two years. "I don't know, Lily. Wish I did." He sighed then forced himself to speak a blunt truth. "Funny, though. That was my thought when I heard suicide. I would ask the captain to speak to a few of them if I had any names." That was actually one of John's better traits. He didn't kiss and tell. "He wanted you and other women and wasn't willing to let go of either fantasy. Maybe that warped flaw hit him at a vulnerable moment." He supposed anything was possible.

"Maybe. God knows I was never enough." She slipped out of his arms and took a step back to gaze up at him. "Captain Carmichael gave me the autopsy results, and the house looked as if he'd either had a party or gone on a drinking binge that night when I came here a few days later."

"Then it's possible things got out of hand. I'm sorry, though. What else can I do for you, Lily?"

Another compassionate gesture or an excuse to see her again, talk to her? Reed didn't answer his own question, having acknowledged eons ago there wasn't much he wouldn't do for Lily, especially when it came to easing the burden her marriage to John had become.

"Right now, I can't think of anything." She laid a hand on his arm, her fingers long and slender, the nails a light pink. "Thank you, Reed. You've been a good friend to both of us. I don't know how I would have coped if you hadn't made sure I knew you were there for me despite John being your friend and partner."

"I'm glad, and that doesn't end now. I want you to feel free to contact me if you need anything, at any time." Her words emphasized what he'd already come to terms with – she would always consider him a friend and nothing more. He understood – he'd seen her at her most vulnerable and witnessed her humiliation at his friend's hands several times. "It's important for you to believe neither I nor any of John's friends have ever approved of his behavior or the way he fought your divorce. It cost him not only you, but several friends, including myself. I regret he didn't get the help we all encouraged him to instead of ending this way, but I hope you'll let the department be there for you as you get things settled." He looked around the house she'd made a home and now owned outright filled with supporting mourners, wondering if she would stay.

Lily averted her face for a second then looked up at him again with a nod. "I appreciate everyone's condolences and support, and I've been over him since moving out, but never bore him ill will. I've made plans to go away for a while, not sure for how long though. Until I can face going through the house and putting it up for sale. Everything is so different from when I would try talking to John about splitting up our assets."

Before either of them could say anything further, two of her closest friends approached with their condolences, and Reed bent down to whisper in her ear. "Anything you need, any time, Lily." He kissed her cheek and moved aside. Lily only had a second to mouth *thank you* with a look of gratitude before accepting her friends' consolation. He nodded and started for the door, unable to stay longer without giving away the jolt of disappointment her announcement about going away gave him. During the first months following John's introduction to his fiancée, Reed had refused to admit his attraction to his friend and partner's soon-to-be wife was anything more than appreciation for a pretty, sweet woman. But the more he was around the couple and got to know Lily, the harder it had become to fool himself.

The only solution, the only way to keep from falling completely for a woman for the first time was to distance himself. John, too enamored of her himself, never noticed when Reed backed off from socializing as much, or how he'd made sure he was never alone with Lily, even for a few moments of polite conversation. Standing as John's best man at their wedding had been torture. He'd gotten drunk afterward, hoping the alcohol would prevent him from fantasizing about having Lily to himself. It was too easy to picture her naked and bound on one of the apparatus in their private play space above Casey's, her pretty breasts or heart-shaped ass pinkened from a long session with his flogger or a spanker, her face suffused with tormented pleasure.

He believed his sacrifices had paid off, and he'd gotten over his adolescent infatuation with his friend's girl. Until Lily had filed for divorce, that surprising move resurrecting the craving for forbidden fruit once again.

Reed pulled his head out of the clouds of wishful thinking and managed to exchange a few words of commiseration with co-workers on his way out, even if he couldn't recall what he'd said to anyone by the time he reached his truck. He didn't mind admitting he wished Lily weren't leaving but wouldn't concede the heaviness pressing on his chest was anything except grief and disappointment over John's death.

Chapter Two

Lily watched Reed walk out, her heart aching, the sour churn of guilt cloying her senses since learning of John's suicide easing somewhat with his partner's support. She wished she had the nerve to call him back, to ask him to stick around and help her get through this day. Reed Kincaid was her closest connection to the man she'd once loved with her whole heart, but she had to learn to stand on her own without the convenience of others to lean on. How many times had those closest to her – her brother, Levi, his girlfriend, Vickie, and her boss, Trina – called her a fool for staying with John after learning of yet another affair? Now that she thought about it, Reed was the only person she'd ever heard call John a fool for his behavior instead of her for putting up with it for so long.

If Reed had been the first person to come to mind whenever she questioned the sanity of trying to make her marriage work instead of moving on, she figured that was normal. As John's partner and friend, Reed had been witness to John's weakness, but he never made excuses for her husband on those rare times he was around during one of their confrontations. Reed's stormy, gray-green gazes and sharp rebukes of John's behavior had gone a long way toward warming Lily where her husband's behavior had left her so cold. She lost track of how often she had compared them, wishing John possessed a fraction of the moral integrity Reed exhibited. And even though he was the first and only man she'd looked at twice since falling in love with John, she could be as wrong about Reed as she'd been about the man she married.

That didn't prevent the memory of what prompted her to consider him as anything more than John's partner from popping up. Four months after finding John in bed with her best friend, Pam, and moving out, she'd returned to the house for another round of arguments and would never forget her response to hearing Reed's deep voice rumble with concern for her, and only her.

She was so upset, Lily's hands shook. Glaring at John from across the living room, her eyes swam with unshed tears of frustration and remorse. His eyes were bloodshot, and his faults did not include heavy drinking. That her actions might have caused him to go off the deep end even once added to the guilt she was already trying to cope with.

"It's been over a long time," she told him again, striving for a calmer tone. "You know it, and I waited too long to acknowledge it. Why can't you admit it?" It was the first time she'd been to their house since moving out four months ago. Having finally ceded the battle of saving her marriage, she thought it only right to give John notice she filed for divorce.

John threw himself onto the recliner, his blue eyes skimming her way before sliding off to the side, as if he couldn't bear looking at her. It was his same reaction each time she had confronted him over an affair in the last eighteen months. She gave him credit for remaining faithful the first six months they were married.

"I believe I was clear when you packed up and left, babe. I'm not letting you go. I made a mistake. We'll deal with it, like always."

"No, John, we won't because we don't deal with it, only I do while you go on your merry way." The hurt from finding John with one of her closest

friends at a Christmas party might never lessen, but it was the last straw for her and had killed what little love she still harbored for her husband. Now that she'd seen the light regarding the end of their marriage, her mistake in holding on for so long couldn't be clearer. Without subjecting herself to her husband's almost daily persuasive remorse, heartfelt promises, and loving gestures, she could admit the utter futility in trying to stay together. "When I found you with Pam, you bluntly stated you weren't going to change because you didn't want to."

He sat forward, looking her way again, his voice turning cajoling, his smile the charming boyish one that had hooked her from the beginning. "Come on, Lil, you know I didn't mean that. I'm crazy about you, babe."

The odd thing was, she believed that last part, which caused her tears to drip. With an angry swipe, she wiped them off her cheeks and snapped, "You never mean anything you say. You have a problem, John. Admit it and get help." Her voice broke on the last word, and she spun around, dashing down the hall to the bathroom as he yelled his annoyed rebuttal.

"God damn it, Lily, we're going to work this

out because I am not signing those fucking papers!"

Leaning against the closed bathroom door, Lily released a shuddering sigh then stiffened when she heard someone else enter the house and start arguing with John. Delicate shivers trickled down her spine as Reed Kincaid's distinctive deep voice filtered through the door.

"Why don't you back off her, Wainscott, give her a divorce, and quit tormenting her? If you care, damn it, do the right thing."

Her brother, Levi, was the only other person she'd heard speak to John that way, but the pleasure of Reed's support was cut short when they started hurling insults.

"Because I'm not giving her up, and fuck you for taking her side," John growled in an even angrier voice than he'd used with her.

"I never thought your callous disregard for women would extend to your wife, whom you keep claiming you love. You're such an ass."

"Right back at you, partner," her husband sneered.

Lily hurried to splash cold water on her face then left the bathroom. The last thing she wanted was to cause a permanent rift in their friendship or work relationship. Reed turned to face her as soon as she stepped into the living area, the several seconds he took to focus his attention solely on her a soothing balm to her frayed nerves.

"You okay, Lily?"

"Of course she is," John answered with exasperation.

Until now, she'd only experienced Levi's overprotective concern, and when Reed spoke to her, ignoring John's frustration with his interference, his simple inquiry filled her with warmth,

"I'm fine, thanks." Lily grabbed her purse, feeling better but ready to put distance between her and John again. "Please sign the papers, John."

Lily pulled her thoughts from the past, noticing her boss arriving. Leave it to Trina to lighten her mood, she thought as the woman who owned Creative Events eyed Reed's backside with a lascivious leer before heading her way. One of the best decisions she'd made since graduating college was to accept the job offer from the event planner. Her boss not only gave Lily her dream job, but the close bond and friendship they now enjoyed was worth just as much.

"That man is such a hunk," Trina said, reaching around Lily to snag a cookie. "*Mmmm*, love these. Have you eaten?"

Lily shook her head. "Not yet, but don't start on me, please. Levi will make sure I do when I wind down."

"Good enough. I've got the Oliver wedding reception, so I can't stay, but I waited until now to tell you I've signed with a temp agency to fill in while you're away. No arguments."

"I don't expect you to hold my job for me indefinitely." She wasn't surprised when Trina insisted on not filling her position when Lily mentioned taking an extended trip. However, with guilt plaguing her from John's sudden death, she didn't need something else troubling her conscience.

Trina ignored her comment, as when she'd uttered the same thing last week, and pulled her in for a quick hug. Always on the move, at forty, her boss possessed an enviable energy level Lily would love to tap into right about now. To admit she was drained was putting it mildly.

"I appreciate you taking a few minutes to swing by. I'm sorry I couldn't help with the back-to-back receptions today." The warm weather months were few and their busiest time for weddings.

"Got it covered. You take care, and call me." With that, Trina breezed out, leaving Lily bereft until Levi and Vickie entered the house several minutes later, returning from making a run for more ice. Levi had been her rock since their parents' unexpected death in a car accident eighteen years ago. She had been only twelve when faced with that devastating loss. If not for her older brother, who had put his life on hold to be there for her, the same as now, she didn't know how she would have gotten through. Back then, he had turned down an overseas journalism opening to remain stateside for her. This time, he had cut short an assignment after Vickie informed him of John's death, returning to Wyoming immediately to see her through yet another loss.

She managed a smile as they carried in the ice and another covered dish, setting it on the table already laden with food. Her brother would never gloat over someone's death, but he must be chafing at the bit to let loose with his happiness that Lily was no longer tied to John in any way. They had argued many times since she'd first learned of her husband's uncontrollable wandering eye. Levi, like so many others, was unable to understand why she'd stayed and tried as long as she had.

Lily spoke a few words to one of John's co-workers before joining Levi and Vickie at the table. "You're going to have to stick around for a month to help me eat all this," she said, nodding at the array of food.

Regret crossed Levi's face. "I wish I could…"

She held up her hand. "I'm kidding. Although, I doubt Vickie would mind."

The two had been together for four years, Vickie the only woman Lily was aware of who had stuck with her brother this long despite all the long absences his job covering hot spots around the world required.

Vickie shook her head, giving him a teasing grin. "We would get on each other's nerves if he hung around all the time."

"Brat." Levi tugged Vickie's short blonde hair, a gesture she didn't seem to mind. "Besides," he told Lily, "knowing you, you already have plans to give most of this to the shelter. None of it will go to waste."

"But freeze that Mexican casserole for when I visit. And some of those brownies." Vickie pointed to a pan of dark chocolate squares then put a finger to her lips. "*Mmm*, and maybe a little of that barbeque…"

"Is Vickie hogging all the food again?"

Lily turned, surprised to see Delia Jenkins, a friendly associate she'd met when she switched to John's pharmacy after getting on his insurance.

Touched by her unexpected support, she replied, "Delia, thank you so much for stopping by, and yes, she's trying to."

Delia met Vickie on one of Vickie's weekend trips to Casper from Cheyenne and joined them for dinner and a movie at her place right after she split from John. Lily had never socialized with the pharmacist but, when she and Vickie had run in to Health Mart and Delia heard about their separation, she had all but invited herself over for a night of support. At the time, Lily and Vickie hadn't appreciated the offer, but Lily found herself grateful that night for the extra shoulder to cry on. She hadn't told anyone the one and only time she'd caught John red-handed had been at the last department Christmas party held at a fellow highway patrolmen's home. She'd gone looking for him and found him in a spare bedroom, screwing Pam, her best friend from college, the only friend she'd stayed close to since graduating, against the wall. The painful double betrayal had been the catalyst she'd needed to end their marriage.

"Nice of you to drop by," Levi stated, his tone neutral, but Lily caught the censure in his gaze.

Frowning at him, she shook her head slightly, just enough for him to know she wanted him to stow his dislike. Levi seemed to forget at times that she was all grown up now and didn't need or want an overprotective guardian. He had approved of very few of her friends during her pre-teen and teen years, and, given he'd only met Delia once, his disapproval was even more annoying.

"I'm sorry I'm a little late, but I overslept then had to get out of this guy's place without waking him." Delia rolled her eyes. "What a loser."

"Maybe you should…"

"Tell me all about him later," Lily interrupted her brother.

For some reason, Delia had rubbed Levi wrong when he had accompanied Lily to the pharmacy on a weekend visit. Once her sibling decided he didn't like someone, there was no getting him to change his mind.

"I will. We're short-staffed today, but I can stay a little while. Do you need anything?" Delia asked with sympathy.

Vickie grabbed Levi's arm and tugged him toward the kitchen. "The crowd has thinned, so we'll get started cleaning up while you two chat."

Giving her a hug, Delia whispered, "I am so sorry, Lil. Now, what can I do?"

During these past months, whenever Lily shopped at the drugstore, Delia had made the effort to ask about her, how she was coping, if there was anything she could do for her. It was much-needed support during a time when she could really appreciate the extra effort from anyone who hadn't betrayed her, even a casual acquaintance like her pharmacist.

"Nothing I can think of, but thank you for coming by."

"Of course." Delia squeezed her hand. "I'll get back to work, then. Let's go to lunch sometime, or do another girls' night."

"I'd like that, but after my trip. I plan to get away for a while, visit relatives."

Delia blinked, as if surprised by that, but then smiled and nodded. "Excellent idea. You need to do something for yourself. You're always doing for others. Give me a call or stop by when you return."

"I will. Thanks."

"I saw Reed Kincaid driving away when we came in earlier," Levi said as he finished drying a plate and handed it to Lily.

Lily reached above her to the open cabinet and placed it on top of the others. That same warm tingle she experienced whenever John's partner had exhibited his unconditional support before and after

John's death returned at the mention of his name. "Yes, he stopped by but didn't stay long. I'm sure it's been hard for him also." She should have asked after him, and now felt bad for letting her own mixed emotions blind her to his grief.

Levi folded the towel in half and laid it on the counter before leaning against it and crossing his arms. Tilting his head, he regarded her with a speculative look. "Did you invite him to stick around?"

"Well, no. I figured he would if he wanted to, and that he must have things to do." She blew out a breath, disgusted with herself. "Thoughtless of me, wasn't it?"

"What?" Vickie asked, entering the kitchen carrying a plate stacked with paper cups that she dumped in the trash. "You're never thoughtless, and often too considerate of others. Don't listen to him." She jerked a thumb toward Levi, who took the gesture and comment with a raised brow.

"Unfortunately, big brother is right. I didn't even ask John's partner how he was holding up."

Vickie released a dramatic sigh and fanned herself. "The all-day five-o'clock shadow does it for me every time."

She flicked Levi a teasing grin, and Lily guessed

her brother's whiskered jaw and mustache also did it for her. Levi frowned, and Lily chuckled for the first time in two weeks, reaching out to pat his shoulder. "If you're jealous, make an honest woman out of her."

"You'll have to take that up with her. Won't she, Vic?"

Lily was familiar with that displeased tone and cast Vickie an uncertain glance, the compact kitchen island separating them. "Sorry. I didn't mean to step on any toes."

"You didn't, but, to be honest, after witnessing your struggles since Levi and I hooked up, I've been gun-shy. You know the saying: if it sounds too good to be true, it likely is." Vickie walked over and hugged Levi, and he unfolded his arms to give her a quick squeeze. "Take it as a compliment and ask me again sometime. I'll let you two chat."

"Get that look off your face and don't worry about us," Levi stated. "We're good. Much better than you and John ever were."

"And now you're waiting for me to say you were right all along?"

Her brother had made his dislike and distrust of John clear from their introduction. She hadn't listened because Levi had done pretty much the same with every guy she introduced him to from the evening of her first date at sixteen. With John, however, his overprotective streak had skyrocketed, she mused, remembering one of his explosive tirades.

Levi threw up his arms in exasperation, the censure and worry in his dark eyes cutting Lily to the quick. "Honestly, Lily, why? The son of a bitch isn't worth your loyalty, let alone one tear. I swear, if he brings you to tears again, I'll pound on his pretty face until no woman will even look at him, let alone sleep with him.

Lily hated disappointing her big brother but couldn't bring herself to give up on John yet, no matter how much his infidelities hurt. "And then I'll have no one because you'll go to prison for assaulting a cop. Please, Levi, respect that I want to handle this on my own, in my own way."

"He's highway patrol, and I don't give a shit, he doesn't deserve your loyalty. Someday, you'll meet someone who will treat you better, and you'll regret wasting so much time and effort on the jackass."

"You don't have to say it. We both know I was right all along," Levi answered, pulling Lily back to the present. "When are you taking off?"

"First thing in the morning, after you and Vickie leave."

Lily hoped the weeks she planned to spend with their relatives in Florida would give her the time and space she needed to come to terms with the guilt of John's death. Everyone, from Levi, to her friends and John's co-workers, had been telling her they'd seen no signs her husband was so traumatized by their impending divorce as to take such a drastic step. Just the opposite, in fact. The night before, Lil and John had enjoyed a much friendlier phone conversation than they had shared in months, and he'd admitted he would always regret losing her but was ready to let go. She hadn't wanted to ruin their friendly talk by mentioning she was aware he'd been seeing someone, and whether it was Pam, her once best friend, or someone new, she didn't know or care at that point.

She worked up a reassuring smile for Levi. "It will be fun to see Aunt Donna again and hang out with our cousins. With their kids, there's a slew of family now. I plan on spending as much time in the sun this winter as I can before returning. Jealous?"

Levi shook his head, wrapped an arm around her in a hug, and replied, "Nope. I'm headed back overseas to finish my assignment. You can send pictures. Night, sis."

He would check the doors for her, so Lily finished wiping down the kitchen then padded into the third bedroom, avoiding the main one she had once shared with John. Levi had been staying here since arriving last week and there was no room in her one-bedroom apartment. She wanted to see him and Vickie off in the morning before closing down the house for her extended absence. There was no one she was closer to than her brother, and with him taking off again, she was looking forward to getting away before she went through everything in the house and put it up for sale.

It sounded corny now, but she'd fallen head over heels in love with John Wainscott at first sight, finding his attentiveness and rakish grin irresistible. He'd wooed her with both over the next six weeks, reeling her in until she answered his proposal without hesitation. For months, she'd been blissfully happy, never doubting he loved her as much as she did him. That surety, along with all the ways he would try to prove the depth of his feelings regardless of his infidelities were one reason she'd stuck it out for so long. His struggles with his failings were difficult to live with, and even more difficult to explain to others who didn't witness them, but also why she'd tried so hard not to give up. Volunteering to help the homeless put her in touch with people suffering from varying addictions, and she'd held out hope John would overcome his weakness for straying to keep her.

Stupid of her, given those words that opened her eyes with a painful sucker punch to the abdomen. *I love you, Lily, but I'm not going to change. I don't want to change,* he had hurled at her when she'd confronted him that night after Pam had fled the room.

Lily boarded a plane two days later, vowing to put her mistakes dealing with her failed marriage behind her before returning to Wyoming.

Seven months later

Trina's blue eyes were shadowed with concern when she flicked her gaze from the house to Lily. "Dare I say congrats?" she asked.

Lily shrugged, a sense of relief filling her from seeing the Sold sign in front of the house she'd once shared with John. "You better. I already spent the equity on my new place," she returned with a wry grin.

She'd thought selling the home she once loved would hurt, but the six months she had spent away from everything and everyone who reminded her of her folly had done wonders. Living with her aunt and uncle and hanging out with her cousins this past winter had shown her what committed relationships were like, what a man meant when he told his spouse he loved her.

The painful words that had revealed the truth and sealed her decision to give up on them no longer haunted her. She had ignored Pam's calls and texts since that night, unable to bring herself to talk to her again with the memory of Pam's face and position with Lily's husband still too easy to recall. Forgiving had come much easier than forgetting. The hurtful words John had hurled at her had driven home the futility of trying to get him to see he needed help. She'd hardened her resolve to get past the shock and devastation he had portrayed when she walked out with her things packed for much longer than a night or two, having allowed his desperate pleadings to sway her for far too long.

"I still don't understand why you bought a place in Eagle's Nest instead of here in Casper."

"I want a change," was all she said, turning her

back on the home she'd once loved. They walked together toward their vehicles parked at the curb. "I appreciate you taking the time after our lunch to do the final walk-through with me."

"You didn't need me, I'm tickled pink to say." Trina nudged her with her elbow, grinning. "I'm thrilled you finally decided to return last month, and that you accepted my partnership offer. We'll make a great team."

"We always have, and just so you know, I'm well aware you dangled that enticing lure in front of me to get me off my butt."

Shrugging without showing an ounce of remorse, Trina opened the Creative Events van door. "Guilty. See you Monday."

"Bright and early. Have a good weekend."

Lily slid behind the wheel of the Mazda SUV she'd purchased in Florida before returning to Wyoming. Having inherited everything from her marriage, including the life insurance John's job with highway patrol provided, had left her able to afford the sporty CX-30, put a down payment on another house, and buy into the partnership with Trina. She wasn't as surprised or as pleased to hear her husband had left her his beneficiary as she was when Trina made the offer to become part owner of

Creative Events. Benefitting from someone's death left her unsettled at first, but Levi had held nothing back when he reminded her of the time, suffering, and finances she had put into her marriage. His no-holds-barred lecture, along with the donations the extra money made possible had helped her accept the money without guilt. The SUV would maneuver well during the snowy and icy winter months when she drove the highway between Eagle's Nest and Casper. And she loved the small Craftsman on the quiet cul-de-sac.

That reminded her of the list of toiletries she wanted to pick up before returning home, and she decided to get them at the drugstore where Delia worked just to say hello. Other than a few texts, she hadn't spoken to anyone besides Trina, Levi, and Vickie while away or since she'd returned, and Lily remembered how Delia had taken the time to come by John's wake.

Lily started the SUV as her phone rang, and surprise held her frozen for a split second when Pam's name and number displayed. She drew a deep breath to dispel the pang tightening her throat then called on her resolve to move on and answered, hoping to put an end to Pam's attempts to talk to her.

"Pam. It's been a long time, and I'm kind of busy."

"I just, look, I moved away for a year right after that party, but now I'm back and still want to see you, apologize face-to-face, and ask if there's any chance we can be friends again. Can we get together, Lily? Please."

It was hard to ignore the teary desperation coloring Pam's voice, but Lily didn't want to revisit the past, not even long enough to hear her once best friend's personal apology. During college, they were joined at the hip, did everything together, including a week of partying on St. Thomas island following graduation. They had led separate lives afterward but made a point of getting together a few times a year until she'd shut everyone out because of John. Maybe Pam had believed that desertion had given her license to encroach; she didn't know or care what the reason was for the betrayal. She didn't have it in her to mend their relationship, preferring to let it go the same as she had John. Now, after everything, the only people she wanted to remain close to were Trina, Levi, and Vickie.

"I've put my marriage behind me, Pam. I've no doubt John pursued you, but you could have said no."

"He did," she rushed to explain, "and I rebuffed him until he came on to me at that house party. I'm sorry. It's no excuse, and I won't say it would have stopped there, because I honestly don't know. He had a way..."

Lily laughed. "I'm well aware of that. I have to go." She hung up wishing that ended their association. Unfortunately, Pam had booked a dinner dance for her parents' fiftieth wedding anniversary through Creative Events while Lily was gone, which meant she would likely be seeing her again at least once. For now, though, she intended to put the call and Pam out of her mind.

After filling a hand basket with first aid supplies and toiletries, Lily walked to the back of the pharmacy where Delia stood facing the shelves of prescription bottles instead of the counter. "Hi, Delia."

Delia's slim shoulders went rigid then she spun around with a wide grin, her cap of short black hair swinging along her jaw. "It's so good to see you! When did you get back?"

"A few weeks ago. I need to restock some over-the-counter stuff for the medicine cabinet and wanted to say hello. I bought a house in Eagle's Nest with a lot more storage than my apartment."

"Did you come by to tell me you're changing pharmacists?" she teased, bracing her hands on the counter separating them.

"No, I like coming in here. Besides, I'll be driving in to Casper for work all the time. It's only a thirty-minute drive from my place in Eagle's Nest." Lily shifted the basket to her other hand, her fist cramping from the tight grip and weight. "You look busy, so I won't keep you."

"I am but how about I meet you for lunch at Ina's in about an hour. I have the rest of the day free. I'd love to swing by and see your house, and hear about your trip. I haven't gotten away in ages and confess I'm jealous."

Lily still had a lot to do at home today but couldn't deny lunch at the popular restaurant off the highway between Casper and Eagle's Nest sounded appealing. "I'd like that. See you soon."

****

"Someone you know?" Allie asked.

Brett shifted his gaze from the two women entering Ina's to his fiancée seated across from him at a corner table. "Lily Wainscott, the brunette with the long hair."

"Wainscott, wasn't that Reed's partner's name?" She paused to eye Lily with more interest before biting into her cheeseburger.

"Yes, and, yes, that's John's widow. Get that look off your face." He'd learned to read Allie very well in the last year, and her expressions always gave her away.

"What look?" she returned, all innocent and sweet.

He wasn't fooled. "Leave it alone. I mean it."

Ignoring him, as usual, she ate a fry then said, "So, she's returned from wherever she went that put Reed in such a funk."

"You don't know that's the reason for his moodiness. I don't even know that. Maybe it's not her. I only met her once at a benefit the highway patrol was sponsoring."

She laughed. "You're sure. I saw the double take you did."

Brett shrugged and picked up the second half of his club sandwich, refusing to confirm her accurate assumption while wondering if Lily would stay or leave again. Reed had only mentioned she was getting away for a while following the wake he had attended, his brother's disgruntled tone telling him a lot. During John and Lily's separation, Reed had mentioned the couple's struggles and his partner's refusal to give up on his wife. He'd gone through a similar trial in ending his marriage, but, unlike Lily, he had filed for divorce as soon as Gina revealed the depth of her greed. It hadn't taken her long to show her true colors once they moved to Wyoming from Texas and she'd seen the extent of his inheritance firsthand.

Allie smirked at him. "Yes, you do, and so does Slade. I've listened to you two speculate about Reed's feelings for her often enough."

Their youngest brother, Slade, didn't mind pushing Brett and Reed to pursue a relationship as long as they left him alone and out of the equation. His hypocrisy wasn't lost on any of them.

"Speculating isn't fact. Are you ready?" He stood and unhooked his Stetson from the back of the chair.

"Yep. Hey," Allie said, taking his hand, "when is our next appointment at Creative Events?"

Brett groaned. "Allie, stop right there." He lifted a hand to Lily seated at a table behind theirs before leading Allie toward the checkout. "Just because Lily worked as Trina's assistant before leaving doesn't mean she's working there now, or even here to stay. Besides, we don't have another appointment until the first of May when we have to finalize our plans. Our wedding is still two months away. Your doing, not mine."

"Yeah, I didn't think that one through."

Her disgruntled tone amused Brett. She was the one who had insisted on waiting almost a year to get to know each other better when he'd proposed a scant month after they had met. He agreed with her decision as they were better suited to make this last now that they were aware of each other's positives and negatives and accepted them without hesitation. The lingering fear from her kidnapping had rattled his thinking last year, the attempt on her life revealing how much he cared for her despite their short acquaintance and the problems his ex had been giving him to get out of their marriage.

Stopping at the register, he reminded her, "Trina, and *maybe* Lily, are likely busy this week preparing for the masquerade charity ball benefitting the new homeless shelter."

Ina Henderson stepped in front of the register from behind the counter, smiling. "We'll be there. Howard's complaining about going as Robin Hood, but I couldn't resist the Maid Marion dress, so he's stuck. Here's your pie."

"Thank goodness for your pies, Ina. Saves me

from baking. I haven't decided on my costume yet, but Brett's being as onery as Howard. Go ahead, tell her," Allie insisted, giving him a poke with her elbow.

Anyone who lived or camped within a fifty-mile radius of Ina and Howard Henderson's block-long mercantile, laundry, and restaurant had shopped or eaten here, and Ina heard all. Having hung out at the ice cream counter in the mercantile as a kid, he'd never seen a reason to keep anything from Ina. "I'm going as Don Juan." There went his plan for complete anonymity.

"Which is cool, except I refuse to go as a lovesick follower. I want a sexy costume, like Wonder Woman."

Ina chuckled at Allie, taking Brett's payment. "You'll be the odd couple. Thanks. See you there."

"See ya, Ina." Brett took Allie's hand and tugged her out the doors, saying, "You did that on purpose because you don't like my costume."

"I sure did."

Chapter Three

"Isn't that one of the Kincaids?" Delia nodded toward the couple leaving the restaurant.

"Yes, Brett Kincaid. His brother, Reed, was John's partner." Lily didn't need to glance that way again to confirm her reply to Delia. Even though she'd only met the oldest brother once, his resemblance to Reed was unmistakable. The warm flash that went through her when she first thought it was Reed was both surprising and unexpected despite thinking of him often while she was in Florida. His close relationship with her husband had made his support for her mean that much more than others from the department.

Delia's expression turned teasing. "That explains the look on your face when you saw him."

Pausing in reaching for her ice water, she asked, "What do you mean?"

"You jolted, flushing before relaxing again, and,

if Reed is anything like his brother, I don't blame you for being attracted."

Lily shook her head in denial, telling herself Delia didn't know her all that well. "Sorry, no. Reed is just as eye-catching as Brett, and nice on top of good-looking, but I haven't been interested in anyone since John."

Cocking her head, Delia's brows dipped in a frown of curiosity. "You're not still pining for John, are you? After everything?"

The waitress arrived with their salads, and Lily waited until she moved away before answering, not surprised Delia, or anyone else would jump to that conclusion. "No, not for a very long time. That doesn't mean I'm ready to get involved again."

Not wanting to discuss either man, she prompted Delia into talking about what she'd been doing while Lily was away. That got them through lunch and as they were walking out to their cars thirty minutes later, she found herself wishing Delia hadn't insisted on stopping by the house, preferring time alone after the busy morning. Since she couldn't find a way to politely turn her down, she gave her the address.

"You can follow me. It's not far once we reach Eagle's Nest."

"Nothing is far apart in that town. It's too small. I don't understand why you moved there. I'll be right behind you."

Lily didn't understand why Delia cared one way or another. It wasn't as if they were good friends, like she and Vickie. Friendly acquaintances described their relationship better. She would never have thought of inviting her pharmacist to a girls' night if Delia hadn't mentioned her love of mystery movies when she overheard Vickie ask Lily which one they were going to choose that night as they stood in line at Delia's counter. Pam used to join her and Vickie on occasion, but that was before she'd proven how weak her friendship with Lily was.

Still, she thought, pulling into her drive with Delia parking behind her, Delia had gone above and beyond in her support before and right after John died. She'd often asked how she was dealing with John's stubborn refusal to acknowledge the end of their marriage and offered an ear if Lily wanted to talk or vent. Before their split, she had been a customer of Delia's and nothing more, and at that time of questioning herself so much and coping with Pam's stab in the back, Lily had been grateful for another hand extended in friendship.

She slid out of her SUV and started toward the

front door, tossing over her shoulder, "Forgive the mess, please. I'm still organizing things."

"This place suits you," Delia said, strolling up the brick walkway with Lily.

"I thought the exact thing when I first drove by. Come in and feel free to look around." Lily closed the door and waved a hand around the living area. "There are two bedrooms and one bath down the hall, and up those narrow stairs is a bonus space. I can look out the window and see for miles."

Delia chuckled and tossed her purse on the wide armchair. "And see what? Fields and cows?"

"I like the view of the rangeland. From my previous apartment, all I saw was a parking lot or buildings." She veered into the kitchen and checked inside the refrigerator before asking, "Would you like something to drink? I have beer, tea, or water." She turned to see Delia gazing at her mystery movie and book collection, the full shelves bracketing the fireplace.

"Tea, thanks. I only saw these that once, but it looks like you've added a few."

Her astuteness surprised Lily, considering she'd only seen the collection that one night last year. "You have a good eye." She padded over and handed her the iced tea. "Books outnumber movies, so I added a shelf in my bedroom." She'd started collecting the mysteries a decade ago, never getting enough of the whodunits. The more one stumped her, the better.

Delia pivoted, her gaze scanning the room before she looked at Lily with a gleam in her eyes. "It's so homey with the quilt draped on top of the sofa, the old-fashioned charm of the place more you than me. I like the arched doorways and rustic mantel though. Thanks for letting me stop in." She drank half the glass and handed it back to Lily. "If I can use your bathroom first, I'll get out of your hair."

"You're not bothering me," Lily rushed to assure her, hoping she hadn't appeared ready to end the afternoon with her company.

"Good to know, but I should get going. I still have weekend errands to run. Maybe we can get together for another movie night now that you're back."

"Sure." Lily walked with her to the door. "I'll check with Vickie and let you know the next time I come by the pharmacy." Vickie preferred it be just the two of them now since they rarely got a free weekend off at the same time. Her job required attendance at a lot of weekend functions booked through Creative Events, and Vickie picked up weekend shifts at hospitals to keep up her nursing while following her dream of writing children's books. But Lily didn't think Vickie would mind if Delia joined them one more time, considering how well they got along before.

"I'd love that, thanks." Picking up her purse, Delia said, "It's nice you have family close. I'm an only child, and, after my parents both passed away, I didn't stay in contact with distant relatives."

Lily couldn't imagine losing touch with any of her relatives. When their parents died so unexpectedly, her aunt and uncle on her mother's side and their paternal grandparents were there for her and Levi. They stayed in frequent contact after Levi insisted on keeping her with him until she left for college, and she remained close to them. She didn't know Delia well but got the impression she didn't get close to too many people.

She waved goodbye from the door and watched her drive away then kicked herself into gear. Lily had never realized how much she and John had accumulated in such a short time until she cleared out the house. At least organizing was a chore she enjoyed.

****

The warm April breeze felt good wafting over Reed's perspiring skin while he watched the calf scamper back to her mother and the herd grazing in their farthest north pasture. He enjoyed spring and the warmth it brought. Winters were long and brutally cold in Wyoming and, come springtime, everyone looked forward to summer's sweat-filled days. Searching for missing livestock among the rougher terrain along the low mountain ridges and in the dense woods was exhausting and not always successful, but luck had been with him and the cowhands today. He eyed the six-month-old Charbray's scraped side from tangling in some thorny bushes and made a mental note to have the calf checked daily until healed.

Neither he nor his brothers knew why their father had chosen the large-bodied, hearty Australian breed to raise here in Wyoming, but Dad liked different, as proven by his blatant, constant womanizing. Being one of the wealthiest cattle and oil barons in the state had often landed Casey Kincaid in the society pages, but his numerous affairs with women who kept getting younger as he aged sealed his notoriety. Growing up with gossip and photos circling around their father and his latest conquest attending a public social function or just out to dinner had resulted in him, Brett, and Slade throwing more than one punch at school recess. The summers they spent running wild on the ranch following their parents' divorce didn't make up for the humiliating ribbing from friends. Turning a deaf ear wasn't as easy as their mother had instructed or portrayed.

Reed nudged Apollo with his booted heels, sending the stallion into a trot toward the lake for a drink before he started back to the ranch. In the last eight months, he hadn't regretted resigning from law enforcement to help Slade run their ranch, which entailed raising eight hundred cattle, a slew of annual crops, and maintaining two productive oil wells. They employed an ample number of cowhands to cover the work, and could easily afford more if necessary, but working alongside his younger brother appealed more to him now than his job with highway patrol had for some time.

Keith, one of four college students Slade had hired at the start of summer last year, reined to a halt alongside Reed. "Hey, boss. Do you want us to drive them south a few miles, closer to the ranch?"

"No, they're fine here for a little longer now that we've found the wanderer." Reed checked on the tan-coated calf again and spotted her grazing next to her mom, appearing calm and content. "She's fine, so we'll head back and you guys can enjoy what's left of the weekend."

Keith's white grin flashed in his sun-kissed face as they turned their mounts. "Jeff and I have hot dates. Sisters. What are your plans?"

Not a date, he thought, almost envying the younger guys their fun. He tried to recall the last time he'd taken a woman out, but, ever since John's suicide left him reeling with guilt, he'd worked from sunup to sunset and only socialized at their play parties on the upper floor of Casey's. He refused to admit Allie's suggestions were correct, that he was pining for Lily's return, even if he wondered on a regular basis how she was doing. When Brett and Allie went into Creative Events to book their wedding, Lily's boss, Trina, had mentioned being shorthanded due to Lily's extended leave. Since he hadn't heard of her return yet, he assumed she was still away, and in the last months, the urge to go to her had dwindled. Nothing, however, seemed to keep him from thinking about her often, too often. He'd never pined for a woman in his life, not even the few he'd developed deeper feelings for. He didn't regret those relationships or the end of them but blamed himself for not noticing John's despair over losing

Lily and the extra pain his suicide put her through.

Reed shrugged then whistled for Evan and Riley to join them before replying, "Hanging out at Casey's, maybe. Slade is scheduled to assist Jordon."

"Do you ever do anything besides go to Casey's on the weekend?" Evan asked, riding up alongside Reed with Riley.

"Sometimes, when the mood strikes for something different. You and Riley going to hang out?" He kicked Apollo into a brisk walk, the others following suit.

"Not this weekend. I'm headed to Cheyenne for my mom's fortieth birthday as soon as we get back. See you at the stable."

"I've got a paper to make up," Riley stated, looking unhappy about spending a Saturday night doing homework. "See you two later."

Evan's mother was young to have a son in college. It was nice hearing the young man's plans as he was not the most responsible when it came to his job. Apparently, his work diligence didn't extend to his education.

"He'll catch up and ace the class. He always does," Keith said.

"I know Slade mentioned giving you fewer hours or days off for schoolwork whenever you need them. Don't hesitate to take them." They rode into view of the barns and stable, the horses prancing in eagerness for a run home. Chuckling, Reed patted Apollo's neck. "Let's go."

Slade strolled over as he dismounted at the corral and looped the reins over the rail. "Found the stray. We'll need to keep an eye on her scraped side for a couple of days. Otherwise, all is good."

His brother's lips curved in a teasing grin that put Reed on alert. "Hold that thought. Allie wants you to come by the house."

They liked it when their soon-to-be sister-in-law kept Brett on his toes, but not so much when she turned her attention on them. He and Slade were happy with their lives, but Allie seemed to think they needed their own happily ever afters now that she and Brett were solid.

"Why? Did she say?"

"Nope." Tugging his hat lower over his brow, Slade's barely there grin kicked up into a wide smile. "But I wouldn't put it past her to track you down, so you may as well go see her and get it over with."

Slade walked away, whistling. He might not care for public socializing, but Slade enjoyed ribbing him and Brett and cutting up with the hired hands he was in charge of as senior manager of the ranch.

Reed finished tending Apollo, removing the saddle and giving him a brush down before turning him out to the pasture to graze. Striding around the stable to his truck, he hoped Allie wouldn't keep him long. He was ready to kick back for a bit before going to Casey's tonight.

He parked in front of Brett's stucco-and-wood-framed house, a few acres separating each of their homes. Despite spending limited time with his sons while they were growing up, Casey had wanted to keep them close, even as adults. Their foreman, Wade Hughes, had done his best to keep them out of trouble while teaching them the work and responsibilities it took to run such a massive spread, and they'd grown to love and appreciate both their inheritance and their father.

Dad would have liked Allie, he mused, ambling up the walk to the front porch to knock on the door. Maybe a little too much, considering her age. The older Casey had gotten, the younger his conquests, right up to his death a few years ago.

"Hey, Reed. Come in." Allie held the door open, smiling. "Thanks for stopping by. Come here. I need a favor."

Uh, oh. He never could resist her when she asked for a favor. Following her into the den, his gaze zeroed in on what looked like Brett's Don Juan costume for the charity masquerade tonight lying on the leather sofa.

"What's up, Allie? Where's Brett?"

She averted her face, another telltale sign she was up to something. "He's delayed with one of his pro bono clients, and I'm not feeling well." Turning a cheeky grin on him, she stated without embarrassment, "That time of the month."

Reed held up a hand, suspecting where she was going with this. "No, I'm not filling in for him. They have your money. That's all that matters."

Allie shook her head then placed a hand on his arm, blue eyes soft and pleading, and damn it, irresistible. "But the Kincaids won't be represented, and you know that's important, Reed. There's no way Slade will go, and that leaves you. Please don't make me be the cause of letting the family down."

His lips quirked with amusement even as his eyes narrowed in suspicion. "Is Brett aware of you changing his plans? And don't lie."

She winced. He didn't need to mention any of the potential, dominant consequences Brett might subject her to if she was trying to pull a fast one for some reason. Allie loved to socialize, and it was unlike her to avoid such events.

"Before he got delayed, I told him I wanted you to go instead. Other than a short text about getting tied up, I haven't heard from him."

That was legit. Brett often took cases at no charge if the client was dealing with harsh circumstances, and anonymity was key to their safety.

"You like these events, so what's the big deal?" she asked. "Did you have plans?"

Reed sighed. He might as well go. Maybe something different tonight would pull him out of his funk. "Just the usual, hanging at Casey's." He went over and picked up the plumed hat and black wig with long braids that would hang down to his chest. A matching mustache and goatee and mask that went over the eyes, nose, and cheeks completed the head pieces, leaving the wide-sleeved white shirt, leather vest that matched the leather pants, a red-lined cape, and a fake sword to complete the ensemble. Holding up the hat, he waved it so the feathery attachment swayed. "You're asking a lot for me to give up my Stetson for this."

She giggled and gave him a hug. "It's for a good cause. Think of all those people you're helping. We'll attend the annual dog walkathon for the shelter next month. Maybe we can find Chance a buddy."

"Chance loves his job herding the livestock,

and he's attached to Slade. Neither would welcome another dog." The border collie's speed, agility, and stamina, not to mention his intelligence, made him the perfect working dog. Reed and Brett had grown just as fond of him as Slade since Slade brought him home a few months ago.

"But you'll go tonight, won't you?" she persisted, her expression hopeful.

"Yeah, what the heck. It might be fun."

"Thank you!" she exclaimed with another hug.

"I'll tell you tomorrow if you're welcome or not," he returned, giving her a quick squeeze before scooping up the outfit. If nothing else, he would enjoy playing a skirt-chasing rogue for a few hours.

"Fair enough. I can't wait to hear all about it."

He still didn't trust the minx's motives but found himself looking forward to the evening after arriving at the Casper Event Center and watching people entering who appeared familiar but were still unrecognizable in their costumes. There were contests for the best costumes and for those who managed to keep their identity secret. The steak dinner catered by one of his favorite establishments was something else that cut into his misgivings about doing this favor.

He'd parked in the rear of the lot in case anyone

arriving recognized his black sporty Mustang with the silver stripe along the sides. After resigning from the highway patrol and turning in his cruiser, he'd opted for the car for personal use, leaving his ranch truck for everything else. Since purchasing the flashy vehicle, way too often he'd pictured Lily sitting next to him as they zipped down the highway with a summer breeze blowing in the lowered windows, whipping her hair around. Not even her extended absence had kept his fantasies at bay for long, and it was past time he set his sights and thoughts to seeing women outside of the few private members of their BDSM group.

With that vow in mind, he went inside and spent a few minutes buying tickets for the raffle drawings, speaking with the volunteers, and looking over the architect's drawings of the renovations they planned for the current shelter. *Lily should be a part of this,* he thought, then put a lid on any further imagining her reaction to the planned improvements.

Striding into the gala room, his resolve to socialize with an interest in hooking up with someone new crumbled the second his gaze landed on the woman welcoming guests. He would recognize that long sable braid and soft profile anywhere, Lily's unexpected presence hitting him with a kick to the gut. She appeared thinner in tan casual slacks and a forest-green blouse, but still soft and appealing. He could still recall the press of her full curves when they'd danced at her wedding, the memory as arousing now as back then. Lily turned with her hand extended, and the same smile he'd fallen for at their introduction robbed him of breath, the instant lust to crush his mouth over her soft lips difficult to stifle.

"Don Juan, right? So far, you're one of a kind." Her breathy voice, free of sadness, washed through him, and Reed returned her smile, taking her hand, waiting for her to recognize him. Instead, she introduced herself as if they'd never met. "I'm Lily Regan with Creative Events. Thank you so much for coming out tonight to help raise money for a new facility for our homeless."

Even in the heels she wore, he stood several inches taller, and Reed glanced down at her name tag to clarify she'd returned to using her maiden name. He debated whether to reveal his identity, not wanting his presence to bring back bad memories. His disguise must be better than he thought. The slight tremor of her hand in his decided for him, and he replied, "My pleasure, Ms. Regan. I'm…"

She hurried to hold up her other hand before

he continued. "Don't tell me your real name, as I'm one of the judges for tonight's contests. You look familiar, but then, everyone does despite the months I've been out of town. Have a pleasant evening."

"Thank you, I will. Nice to meet you."

She stiffened and peered at him closer before shaking her head, as if his voice jarred a memory. "It'll come to me."

"When it does, let me know."

Reed moved on, the motive for Allie's change of plans now clear. He should be glad Lily didn't recognize him or his voice right away.

Should be, but he wasn't.

That meant she'd given him little thought since they'd seen each other at John's wake, unlike his inability to stop thinking about her. That didn't surprise him, he admitted. She'd never viewed him as anything more than her husband's friend and partner, either while married or after they had split. That should make it easier for him to move on also.

Should, but it didn't.

Twenty minutes later, Lily strolled behind a microphone and announced the last call for cocktails before dinner was served. "Thank you," she added before her gaze connected with his, the deep breath she sucked in lifting her chest, her face turning pink with interest. A hot surge of blood pumped into his cock, the last response he needed to get through the night when he couldn't keep his eyes off her. He turned away to continue conversing with a group of ranchers, deciding it would be best if he revealed himself the next time they crossed paths tonight, regardless of how she felt about him, and then make an early night of it. The shelter already had the Kincaids' sizable donation.

But, between her disappearance into the kitchen during dinner, and then her responsibilities before the raffle drawings commenced, the opportunity to speak again never materialized. Reed struggled to focus on conversations and activities, most revolving around guessing identities, while cursing Allie for not warning him about Lily's return. He couldn't seem to keep his eyes from straying her way or tamp down his response each time she met his gaze with a curious look of barely concealed interest.

At first, she appeared happy and sociable, laughing with guests, much more relaxed than that last day, when she was mourning John's passing. He assumed both the months away and the coroner's final report of accidental overdose helped the most.

Reed wished he could say the same for him, but his reaction to seeing her again, touching her, and hearing her voice stirred that forbidden need to life, proving he wanted her as much now as before. Her gaze cut his way as often as he sought her out, and if he were dumb enough to read more into that than was wise, like she was looking for him, he deserved the tight clutch in his groin whenever their eyes connected. As attuned as he was to Lily, he noticed the pleasure suffusing her face disappearing when a woman dressed as Cinderella approached her. Even from across the room, he could make out her tight lips and pale face, the way she shook her head against whatever the other woman was saying, how her shoulders slumped as the woman walked away. The change in her made it much harder to keep his distance.

****

"Can we talk?"

Lily backed away from Pam, the first person she recognized right off in costume. Seeing her again resurrected old memories she'd hoped were buried for good and would no longer hurt. "I didn't know you would be here tonight." She winced at her accusatory tone, a stab of guilt poking her when Pam blanched.

"I wasn't sure if you were privy to the guest

list. Please, Lily. I just need you to let me apologize. John...damn, he had a way..."

She shook her head, pain mixed with anger gripping her abdomen in a vise. "I'm well aware of his talented persuasion. Look, I'm working, and this is neither the time nor place."

"I know, I know, but you wouldn't talk to me after that Christmas party and didn't respond to the note I put in my condolence card, and then you were gone. I'm not asking for forgiveness, just a chance to..."

Lily took another step back, needing to put space between them. John's last deflection hadn't hurt her as much as her friend's betrayal, and she realized she wasn't coping as well as she'd believed with Pam's disloyalty.

"I'm not holding a grudge, Pam. I only want to put all that behind me. You are a reminder of what he put me through." The disappointment of learning she wasn't as immune to that hurt as she'd thought put a damper on the festivities.

Pam's heavily made-up face fell, her eyes turning teary as she nodded. "How about a late breakfast tomorrow? Would you at least consider that, just to sit down and talk? I need that, even if you don't."

The right thing, the cleansing thing to do would be to forgive and forget, but during the volatile up-and-down years she spent with John, she'd lost touch with her closest friends except Pam. Her family's love and support when John's cheating cost her that friendship had been all she needed, and all she wanted now.

"I can't. I'll be at the shelter tomorrow." Lily didn't offer to meet her after she finished helping serve the noon meal at the homeless shelter. A look of frustrated anger replaced Pam's remorseful expression, prompting Lily to hurry and say, "Have a good evening. Thanks for coming."

The last hour of the event dragged on for Lily as she strove to maintain a happy face while all the heartache, humiliation, and wasted time and effort over her marriage came rushing back. She searched for Don Juan again, hoping her interest in the stranger, a first for her, would restore her earlier good mood. Like the other times this evening when she'd sought him out, her pulse jumped upon picking out his tall frame in the crowd. Spotting him with his head bent low over a woman draped in a sexy Cleopatra gown, the two laughing, a ripple of envy shot through her. She wished she possessed the nerve to flirt openly like that with him. He reminded her of Reed Kincaid, despite the long cape that hid most of his build and the mask, goatee, wig, and hat that left his features hidden. With luck, this sudden interest in a man was a good sign she was over the mistakes she'd made with John. When he checked her name tag in the greeting line and called her Ms. Regan without a hint of recognition, she realized it was her imagination spurred by her inability to forget about him that made her compare Don Juan to Reed.

Lily started to turn away, lecturing herself to stay focused on the job, not Pam, John, or a sexy guest, but he looked up, and they shared another long, potent moment. She jolted, heat unfurling deep inside her long-neglected pussy, the same reaction as every other time when their attention zeroed in on each other in the past two hours. It wasn't enough to restore her previous good mood, but something to occupy her mind while finishing her job.

Chapter Four

Lily joined the other volunteers at the long table holding the raffle prizes, relieved her duties were coming to an end. The caterers had left and once the event center's staff came in to clean up shortly, her job would be done. She only listened with half an ear to the director of the shelter's thank-you speech, hoping the drawings wouldn't take long. Thinking of Don Juan as *her* Don Juan this past hour hadn't been enough of a pleasant fantasy to dispel her morose mood, but at least it steered her thoughts away from painful memories.

The shelter's director announced the first winner and kept drawing until a short line had formed to pick up their prizes. Over a hundred baskets, gift cards, small electronics, and free services were donated, and Lily's concentration was on putting the right prize in the right outstretched hand, not the face that went with the hand until her fingers tingled from the brush of a man's large calloused palm. Her gaze flew up, and she went hot when she encountered Don Juan's slow smile and was once again struck by the resemblance to Reed. He still wore the hat that shielded his eyes behind the mask, so she was left guessing he might be a relative. Before she could ask, the line shifted, and he nodded, tipped his hat, and walked off.

For the first time, she experienced what it meant to feel alone in a room with other people, her bereft mood plummeting further as he walked away. Lily excused herself from the small group of volunteers once the final prize was given out and the last of the guests were leaving, including her Don Juan. Oddly let down when he didn't wave or acknowledge her in any way, she slipped out onto the surrounding patio. The music turned off, and she figured it would take about fifteen minutes for the shelter personnel to gather their things, clearing the way for cleanup.

The cooler air relieved the stuffiness from the crowded room, and she settled against the wall around the corner, the semidarkness more fitting to her mood. Lily could kick herself for letting Pam's unexpected presence trouble her so much after she'd thought she had put all that behind her for good. She couldn't wait to get home and indulge in a big glass of wine and crawl into bed, maybe fantasize about a sexy stranger stripping off his costume and joining her. That was the extent of her sex life since leaving John, the last man she'd slept with.

God, had it really been almost two years? No wonder she was growing warm just from eyeing strangers.

Laughter drifted from the parking lot to her secluded nook around the side, and she wondered how much longer it would take to get over the stupidity of trying to make a hopeless marriage work. At least she'd looked at a man with interest tonight. That definitely went in the plus column toward getting over her failure with John. A torrid one-night stand with a stranger might be the antidote she needed, if only...

Heavy-booted footfalls pulled her attention out of the clouds a second before the tall, broad-shouldered Don Juan appeared a foot away. Lily gasped in startled awareness, heat enveloping her from head to toe as he stepped closer, his big body enclosing them in the dark corner.

His breath fanned along her cheek in a warm caress as he whispered, "Are you okay?"

Lily couldn't fathom why he would think otherwise, but the thoughtfulness behind the inquiry and rough rumble of his deep voice ignited the slow burn of need that had been coiling low in her abdomen all night. Raw, primitive lust grabbed hold of her body and common sense, deeper, stronger than she'd experienced when she'd fallen for John. A reckless abandonment gripped her, an ache for pleasure to replace the resurgence of self-recriminations.

Before she chickened out, she hastened to reply, "What...what if I said no?"

He'd draped the long cape over his arm, and she could detect the tightness of his body with her answer, unsure if that was a good sign until he cursed, dropped the cape, and pressed his rock-hard body against her. His head swooped down and he crushed his mouth over hers, kissing her with rough possession, his lips hard and searching, inflaming her senses. The degree to which she responded stunned her, her pussy spasming, filling with liquid heat as she gripped his thick biceps to anchor herself against the frenzied storm of unleashed emotions and lust.

The fake goatee scratched her chin, the plastic mask pressing against her cheek and nose as he slid his hands behind her, one gripping her nape, the other taking firm hold of her buttock. Lily moaned, opening for his tongue, grateful for the dark and his total control that offered so much freedom to just *feel*. She forgot everything that had come before this stolen decadent moment, the first daring, shameless risk she'd ever taken. His fingers dug into her cheek, holding her pelvis against his throbbing erection as he kneaded her buttock. New sensations erupted across her backside, hot licks of pleasure seeping into her pussy, his lips turning even more aggressive moving over hers.

Lily was so swept up in the rising tide of arousal consuming her, she didn't notice when he released her nape and opened her blouse until cool air brought goose bumps to her upper chest. She whimpered as a calloused finger slipped inside her bra and brushed her nipple, a shiver racking her body, her only cognizant thought – *more*. Arching into that finger, she drew her hands up to his broad shoulders, the plumes hanging from his hat tickling her fingers.

The virtual stranger eased up, lifted his mouth off hers, and a desperate plea escaped before she could stop it. *"Please."*

It was his turn to groan, and she basked in the low vibration, enjoying that he seemed as affected as her. He lowered his mouth again, feathering light kisses across her cheek and down her neck, his teeth sinking into the sensitive spot where shoulder met neck, the sharp nip accompanying the scratch of his nail across her nipple. Lily shuddered from the dual pinpricks, and the surprising up-kick of arousal they elicited. She couldn't see a thing but leaned her head against the wall and closed her eyes anyway. Somehow, that made it easier to let go with the strange response to discomfort instead of wasting precious time questioning it.

His breath grew harsh against her neck, his finger abandoning her breast as he took his hand down to her waist, flipped open the button on her slacks, and lowered the zipper. Sucking in a raw lungful of air, she braced for an even more intimate touch, craving it despite the sane part of her repeatedly asking if she'd lost her mind.

He nipped the soft flesh of her upper breast, his hand sliding into her loosened waistband far enough for his fingers to graze her labia. "Yes?" he questioned above her lips, his hold on her buttock tightening yet again.

Lily nodded, the heightened arousal his touch had unleashed both exciting and scary, the combined tumult between her emotions and body rendering her speechless. Slamming his lips over hers again, he drove inside her spasming pussy, the one deep thrust enough to set off small contractions of damp release. Her body overruled the last of her disbelief and usual common sense, attempting to arch closer, urge him to move faster, bring her to the peak that had become essential before he disappeared from her life. But his control kept her pelvis still, her pussy fluttering then convulsing as he took hold of her clit and pumped the tender bundle of nerves. Wrenching her mouth away from his, she gasped a much-needed breath that caught on a whimper, the all-consuming pleasure ripping through her body rendering her dumbfounded with the swift rise and intensity.

Awareness resumed by slow degrees, the light play of his fingers soothing Lily's shivering until another curse spilled from his mouth, his large frame going rigid as he removed both hands from her body. "Shit, what the hell am I thinking?" Before she could assimilate the change in him, he did up her slacks and took one step back. "I'm sorry. This... it wasn't right. You don't...never mind. I'm sorry."

The abruptness of his departure was as shocking as his quiet, unexpected arrival. She stood there with her lips and nipple throbbing, her pussy damp, aching for another touch, his hard hands and gentle hold, the press of his big body, his warm breath…

Lily gathered her wits enough to peek around the alcove and watch him walk away. Another wave of familiarity struck her when he strode into the meager glow from the wide patio doors, the view of him from the rear reminding her of someone. Then he turned the corner, reaching up to sweep off his hat, along with the wig and mask. She jerked in recognition, gasping at the brief glimpse of his profile.

Reed.

****

Reed tossed the cape, hat, wig, and mask into the back seat, got into his car, and slammed the door, calling himself every kind of fool. He'd done the right thing all evening by staying away from Lily after realizing she didn't recognize him. Not since they'd first met and during those early months of her marriage had he seen her so relaxed and happy, her smiles natural instead of forced. Revealing his identity would only remind her of John and the hell his partner put her through, and he refused to risk putting a damper on her fun or distracting her from her work.

Then his good intentions had gone out the

window when her short conversation with a woman dressed as Cinderella had deflated her expression, causing her face to appear brittle with hurt and ill will. He didn't recognize the other woman but caught her glare aimed at Lily's back when she turned away from her.

One glimpse at the regret clouding Lily's face and the brief, barely there touch of their fingers as he'd accepted his raffle prize had been his final undoing, and he'd followed her outside just to check on her. Lily's whispered *please* still echoed in his head, her soft, shaky voice crumbling the last of his resolve.

Turning on the ignition, Reed cursed his weakness and idiocy. What amounted to minor foreplay for him, and he drove home with a raging hard-on for a woman who had never viewed him as anything more than a friend. He couldn't recall another woman who left him yearning for the soft yielding of her body to his control, her breathy moans filling his mouth, or the ripple of her orgasm around his fingers. He pictured Lily naked on his bed, maybe with her hands bound above her, her face reflecting a need for him, and only him. It would do no good to speculate whether she would enjoy a visit to their private play room above Casey's, regardless of the way she'd surrendered to his possessive hold in that dark corner. His relationship with John and intimate knowledge of her husband's philandering would be a constant reminder, not to mention she'd never even hinted at an interest in him, or any other man that he was aware of.

Reed was more than ready to get home and turn in for the night, but, when he noticed the barn's loft light still shining in the one upper window, he stopped there first. His concern switched from Lily to Slade, who was often plagued at night with memories of his past stint as an Army sniper. He'd never shared details of the deaths the government ordered him to execute, or the reason for his abrupt resignation, only telling Reed and Brett the ends didn't always justify the means. He felt for his brother. During his years in law enforcement, Reed had seen enough of the worst of humanity and the consequences of their actions on innocent people to last him a lifetime.

As he'd thought, he found Slade seated on the edge of the loft's open double doors with one leg bent, his arm resting atop his knee as he whittled on a piece of wood. Reed walked across the upper floor with hay bales stacked on both sides and leaned sideways, his shoulder braced against the wall, looking down at Slade with crossed arms.

"You're up late."

"Right back at you," Slade returned without taking his eyes off the carving.

"True. I'll share if you will."

Slade huffed a laugh. "Don't need to. You're so fucking easy to read. Heard John's widow has returned."

Reed sighed, making sure he didn't lean forward far enough to get dizzy from the height. He figured Slade's ease with sitting in that open, elevated space stemmed from the hours he'd spent perched in a tree or on a hilltop, waiting to get a bead on his target. "And?" he asked, wishing his brothers would limit their keen astuteness to the subs in their play group.

"Come on, Reed." Slade glanced up at him. "You've walked around with a hard-on for that woman for as long as you've known her."

"I don't take after our father, the same as you and Brett," he snapped. Casey had been a notorious womanizer, the younger the better, regardless of their marital status, if he wanted them. To this day, he didn't know how their mother stayed with him for ten years.

"Don't get bent out of shape. I didn't say you acted on your feelings, did I? But she's free now."

Recalling the change in Lily when speaking with the woman in the Cinderella costume, he couldn't help thinking John's philandering was once again causing her grief. If so, she wasn't free of the past at all.

"Some hurts you can never set aside." Dropping his arms, he started toward the ladder, tossing over his shoulder, "You have experience with that."

Thirty minutes later, Reed fell into bed vowing to leave Lily alone and find someone else to fixate on, or a new member of their private group to get better acquainted with. But, first thing tomorrow, he planned to have a little chat with Allie.

****

Lily still shook with ripples of pleasure and her uncharacteristic behavior that led to that off-the-charts orgasm when she turned to go inside, her thoughts staggered by the realization of who had gifted her with that much-needed release. She remembered stopping Reed from revealing his identity in the greeting line, so she couldn't blame him for keeping quiet then. And they both had participated in exchanging silent, pulse-jumping moments separated by the crowd throughout the evening, a new experience for her on top of succumbing to a stranger for the first time. She didn't understand why he kept his identity secret when he joined her outside but was oddly grateful he had. Knowing who she'd been drawn to all night and aware of his dominant sexual practices, not to mention his close relationship with her husband and their marital issues, she likely would not have let go like that. She couldn't bring herself to regret the encounter yet, even if she doubted the rendezvous was anything new for Reed.

John used to tease her about joining the Kincaids' private group of friends who were into the alternative sexual practices she'd heard and read a lot about. She never thought anything of Reed's personal life, at first, too crazy about John and, later, too hurt and disillusioned to reflect on any man or care about his sexual proclivities. But now, after her rash behavior led to experiencing Reed's touch, his controlling hold, and the benefits of both, she couldn't think about anything else. His identity helped her reconcile why she had trusted him as a stranger, figuring a part of her recognized the man who had stood for her against his friend and partner. She wasn't miffed at the deception, too grateful at the moment for the euphoric experience and ensuing pleasant mellowness replacing her earlier disheartenment.

Hoping no one noticed her short absence while the guests were leaving, Lily slipped back inside and tried to concentrate on finishing her job. The food caterers wasted no time packing their van and leaving, and, once the custodians took over, she followed the last of the venue's staff out to the parking lot.

"Good night," she called out to the two women getting into the only other car in the lot as she went down the front steps.

"Night, Lily."

Lily watched their taillights as she strolled to her Mazda, the click of her heels on the pavement echoing in the shadowy silence now encompassing the empty space. A frisson of unease skated down her spine as she pressed the unlock button on the car fob and reached for the door handle. A masked, cloaked figure charged at her out of nowhere, both arms raised, hands gripping a baseball bat. Startled, her heart jumping to her throat, and she screeched and ducked, the assailant's swing bouncing the bat off her shoulder before smashing through the car door window.

A genderless chuckle reached her ears from behind the grotesque face covering at the same moment the venue's security guard shouted, "Halt right there!"

Fast-running, hard-pounding footfalls resonated through the roaring of fear in her head, and Lily managed to straighten her trembling legs. She glimpsed the flying tails of the long cloak as her attacker dashed around the end of the building, unable to make out enough to describe to the police.

"Are you all right?" the guard asked, eyeing her with concern.

"Yes, just...*whew!*" She brushed the back of her hand across her damp forehead. "A bit unnerved."

"Well, I'm more than a bit. I'm so sorry. I headed this way as soon as I saw the custodians arrive. Police are on their way. Here." He opened her car door and took her elbow. "Sit down until they... there they are now."

Lily sank onto the seat, the sirens dwindling when the police pulled into the lot. She didn't get a good look at the disguised mugger and hadn't been able to tell if the brief snicker she heard was male or female. Exhaustion pressed down on her, her shoulder throbbed, and all she wanted was to go home and bury herself under her grandmother's quilt but doubted she would sleep after that unexpected scare.

Squeezing her hands together, Lily drew a deep breath to help steady her nerves, wishing now Reed had stuck around a little longer. His calming, supportive presence would be worth a little embarrassment. There was always time later to question his motives behind remaining incognito.

"Ms. Regan, are you up to giving a statement?"

Nodding at the police officer, Lily stood, determined to put this behind her as fast as possible and not allow one random incident to affect her life.

Lily's assailant crouched behind the wheel, filled with glee watching the Mazda pull out of the lot. Spooking the woman who was responsible for screwing up her perfect life was as much fun as plotting new ways to torment her. If not for her, John would still be alive, and she would pay for causing his death…and pay…and pay…

****

Reed awoke with a piss-poor attitude that was more Slade on a bad day than himself at his worst. With the temperature forecasted in the low seventies and few chores waiting, he should be looking forward to a ride with his brothers before heading to their mom's for Sunday dinner. Instead, the restless night plagued with worrying about Lily beating herself up for letting go with a stranger left him edgy and irritable. He dressed and downed coffee, working at improving his mood before confronting Allie. It wouldn't do for him to alienate Brett by going off on the woman he had prodded his brother into taking a chance on.

Before he reached Brett's house, he came across him scowling at the flat tires of his truck. He stopped and got out, nudging his Stetson up to eye the deflated front tires. "Two at the same time?" he asked, understanding Brett's thunderous expression. "What happened?"

Brett, standing next to the opened driver's side door, pointed downward. "Take a look."

Peeking under the vehicle, he saw a strip of nails, the sharp points facing upward, lying across the main drive that connected to all three of their homes and the barns. "There's no way that was left by accident." Infuriating. The heavy-duty, oversized tires needed to drive the trucks over rough terrain weren't cheap.

Fists planted on his hips, Brett drawled sarcastically, "No kidding."

"Don't get cranky with me. I'm already annoyed with your fiancée."

Brett's face switching from aggravated to surprised to suspicious. "What'd she do?"

Reed leaned against his truck and folded his arms, recalling his shock at seeing Lily again without any warning she had returned or would be handling last night's event. A heads-up would have gone a long way in changing how the evening had gone. "Did you know John's widow, Lily, was back in Casper and working again at Creative Events?"

Brett looked confused. "We saw her recently at Ina's, and Trina mentioned once her assistant would return soon, so I assumed Lily was back at work there. What does..." Enlightenment dawned. At least his brother wasn't in on Allie's manipulations. "*You're* the one she talked into going last night in our place? All she told me was she didn't feel well."

"Yeah, me, too. She *didn't* mention Lily though." Reed straightened and tugged his hat back down. "Get in, and we'll call for tires to be delivered tomorrow, which is about all we can do on a Sunday."

"Aren't you going to elaborate on last night?" Brett got into the truck and shut the passenger-side door.

Reed didn't have to think twice about his answer. "No, and tell Allie to butt out. Please."

"Oh, no worries there. I'll even let you watch."

Chuckling, he put the truck in gear and started for the stables, saying, "She would like that part." As long as Brett was focused on Allie, she didn't care who else was around, at least not when they were holding a private play party above Casey's.

They arrived at the stable at the same time Slade pulled up astride his motorcycle. He removed his helmet and said, "I just saw your truck. What gives?"

"You must not have noticed the strip of nails responsible for the flats. Deliberate, we're thinking." Brett's gaze cut to Evan and Jeff who were cleaning out the horse trough in the corral. "When did they get here this morning?"

Slade glowered. "Are you accusing them of something?"

Reed interjected. "No one's accusing the kids of anything, but you never discovered who was responsible for the destroyed property last summer. And then there was the ruined feed incident in January."

During a heavy snow pileup, someone had snuck into the large barn and ripped open the stored feed bags, spreading grain and shredded burlap all over the floor. That many destructive pranks weren't a coincidence and reeked of an inside perpetrator.

As senior manager of the Soaring Eagle Ranch, Slade was in charge of the hired hands and protective of the young college guys interning with him.

"It's not teenage pranks," Brett said, his tone softer.

"Maybe, but I'm not firing anyone on a suspicion." Slade swung a leg around and got off the bike, raking his fingers through his hair. "Mom doesn't like my bike, so I'm riding with you to dinner. William asked to grill fish, so I suggest we get out to the lake and back pronto if we want dinner this evening."

Their mother, Andrea, had chosen well when she remarried. William doted on her and was faithful, two big pluses in all three of their eyes.

Brett nodded. "Allie's making mac and cheese from scratch. Let's stow our pissy moods and enjoy the day."

"I'm good with that," Reed agreed, striding toward the stable. "But I'm still going to have a word with her. After mac and cheese."

They murmured quietly behind him as he went to Apollo's stall, Slade's louder response of, "Can I watch?" making him laugh.

****

The opportunity for that word with Brett's fiancée presented itself after Sunday dinner. Reed followed Allie out to the backyard while Brett and William were still engaged in legal talk and Slade was helping their mother with dishes. All through dinner, he continued to think about Lily's peace of mind after last night, imagining her astonishment over her behavior and the shock of her response still lingered today. He continued to struggle with his actions and knew from experience he would have to check on her himself to settle his conscience, and planned to do so when he found her new address.

Andrea and William's new puppy, a rambunctious Goldendoodle, ran circles around Allie where she stood in the yard laughing. Reed couldn't help but find them both amusing and paused on the patio until Allie noticed him. She winced with a spasm of guilt then strolled toward him with a flirty grin.

"How mad are you?"

Reed fisted his hands on his hips and cocked his head as she stood before him. "On a scale of one to ten, six."

"That's not too bad. It must have gone okay."

She didn't sound the least bit remorseful, but that was Allie. She didn't spare a second for regrets, calling it a waste of time. "Sweetheart, what were you trying to do, get us together? That's not happening."

"Why?" she returned bluntly.

Why? Because Lily had loved his friend and partner so much she had worked to save their marriage far longer and during the most painful of betrayals than anyone else would have. Most people would call her efforts ridiculous; some would say admirable. He only ever wanted her to be happy.

"Stay out of things you don't understand." He hesitated then added, "Please."

"Okay." Allie laid a hand on his cheek for a moment, her blue eyes now shining with compassion. "I just want Brett's brothers to be as happy as he is, and I am."

She dropped her hand and went inside, leaving him to brood alone until the back door opened again and his mother joined him. The puppy, Brandy, dashed over, and Andrea scooped her up then thrust the wriggling bundle of cinnamon curls into his arms.

"If she can't bring a smile to your face, nothing can. What's on your mind today, Reed?"

He blew out a breath and shook his head, rubbing Brandy's neck and trying to avoid her lapping tongue reaching for his face. "Okay, enough.

Down you go." Bending, he released her to chase a butterfly then gave his mother a rueful glance. "How did I go from having no women invading my thoughts to three?" He realized his mistake the moment her eyes widened and a wide grin blossomed.

"Three? Me you've endured for almost thirty-nine years. Now there's Allie, she's so cute..."

"Sometimes not so cute," he cut in.

Andrea looked inside the glass doors then back at Reed with a frown. "Surely you're not upset with her? I'm positive whatever she said or did, it was with a good heart."

"No, I'm not upset with her." Well, maybe a little. His mother was right though, Allie's intentions are always good.

"Is the third someone special?" she persisted.

Images ran through Reed's head: Lily getting out on a cold, snowy day to coax a homeless woman into shelter, her face filled with compassion; Lily devastated by John's latest betrayal, her eyes showing the first hint of resignation about ending her marriage; Lily quivering in his arms last night, her soft nipple going stiff under his touch, her pussy fluttering around his fingers, her quick, damp orgasm damn near hindering his circulation. Special didn't begin to describe her.

"Yes and no, and that's all I'm saying." He bent and kissed her cheek. "But I love you for caring."

She squeezed his shoulder, replying, "Just remember I'm here if you need me. All I ever wanted for you boys is for you to be happy."

Reed recalled thinking the exact same thing about Lily then pivoted and followed his mother inside.

Chapter Five

"You did what?"

"Shhh!" Lily gripped her phone, hurrying to keep Vickie's voice down. "Don't let Levi hear you!"

She'd made it through the week without telling anyone about those stolen moments with Reed last Saturday, but with a free weekend ahead of her and nothing to do except continue to curse and savor her first illicit tryst, she'd succumbed to the need for some unbiased input. And who else would she confide in besides Vickie? During her separation and the months spent in Florida, she'd isolated herself from everyone except family and working with Trina. There were some things, though, she couldn't share with her boss, like improper engagements while working for a client.

"Relax. He's packing to leave early tomorrow. I can't believe it, you and Reed Kincaid. Damn, girl, you couldn't have picked better to dip your toes into the man pool again. If I didn't have Levi, I'd hate you right now."

Lily smiled, rotated her still-sore shoulder, and sank onto the couch. Leave it to Vickie to ease her tension with a few words. "Then I'm doubly glad you have my brother."

"But I'm free this weekend and I'll be at your door before lunch. Make plans, and I want details, *specific* details."

"In that case, I'll run out in the morning for wine. See you tomorrow."

She hung up, relieved to have company for a night or two. Between second-guessing her unprofessional, uncharacteristic behavior and coping with the trauma of a vicious mugging attempt, she doubted she had managed more than a few hours' sleep each night in the past week. The thought of going out alone after nightfall drew a shiver down her spine, a clue to how much that attack had affected her. To take her mind off that scare, she would play the moments spent in that dark corner over and over in her head. The mental rewind never failed to chase away the cold fear with a warm rush, similar but less intense to what she experienced that night.

Lily padded over to the front window and closed the drapes, figuring the impact of both memories would fade soon and then disappear. Then life would go back to normal. When that depressed her, she picked up her latest mystery novel, flicked off lights on her way to her bedroom, and propped herself against her white-wicker headboard to read until she fell asleep.

Vickie arrived as Lily finished stuffing the croissants with chicken salad but refused to wait until after lunch to start talking about last weekend. Dropping her overnight bag next to the kitchen chair, she hugged Lily before saying, "Hi, good to see you again, now begin where you left off. He found you on the patio at a vulnerable moment and…"

"Hello to you also," Lily returned, amused and grateful for Vickie's way of opening an awkward conversation. "Let's sit on the patio. It's too nice to stay indoors." She carried the plates out the back door off the kitchen and set them on the round wood table she'd picked up at a garage sale. Sitting down across from Vickie, she took a bite before replying, "Disguised as Don Juan, he proved too irresistible for my common sense to refuse, and I admit I don't regret the encounter. In all honesty, it helped not knowing his identity. Maybe I figured, why not? This way, I wouldn't have to worry about an awkward surprise meeting later." She went on to describe how she discovered his identity and then told her about the cloaked mugger.

Putting down her sandwich, Vickie glared at her. "You did not mention an attack to Levi. He would have told me."

Lily grimaced. She should have told her brother but needed time to get over the scare before dealing with him on her doorstep within a few hours of hearing about it. His overprotective streak had gotten her through the unexpected death of their parents and sensitive teenage years, but she preferred coping with life's trials on her own, without leaning on others. Besides, it was a random attack that could have happened to anyone in that guy's path, not a personal affront. She *would* put it behind her, and soon.

"I'll tell him," she assured Vickie. "When I'm sure my voice won't wobble. Now, do you want to continue glowering at me or hear those details?"

"I'll settle for the details on both after I remind you how pissed Levi was when you waited over a year to tell us about your problems with John. You admitted you've never seen him so mad, and you tend to bottle up when stressed. Okay, now go." Vickie bit into her croissant, never taking her eyes off Lily as she unloaded.

Lily didn't want to think about Levi's wrath

when she couldn't keep silent about John's infidelity any longer, so she talked about the best part of that night first. "Between you and me, I now understand the excitement of anonymous trysts. I'm not kinky, but, God, Vickie, even the best sex with John can't compare to those few moments. And he didn't even...you know, he only..." She reached for her iced tea and downed a long gulp, embarrassed.

Vickie laughed. "You should see how red your face is! And no, not from the sun shining on us. I get it – touching, no intercourse. Did he get you off?"

Lily went hot again but couldn't hold back from her friend's prodding. "Like a firecracker. His mouth muffled my mortifying whimpering, something I've *never* done."

Sex with John had been great until she'd become aware of his extracurricular activities. After that, she tried but couldn't relax enough or keep from wondering who he was thinking about when they were together to achieve that heightened pleasure again.

"Then you weren't with the right guy. Hey, I think it's great, Lil. Any up close and personal time you can get with a guy, you ought to go for. You're long overdue. But I have to say, after you shocked me yesterday with what happened, I half expected you to greet me today unnerved or exhibiting signs of delayed remorse, disbelief at your atypical behavior, or making excuses, like calling it a stupid mistake. You're not a flirt, and there'd been no one since you first met John, right?"

"No, I always thought John was the one and only, and it's been hard letting that dream go. But I gotta tell you, the way Reed took over in a nonaggressive manner liberated me from all misgivings." That memory would fade, but, until then, she would savor her impulsive taste of decadence.

"John's actions crushed your self-esteem, and I'll bet having a stranger's attention felt damn good," Vickie stated. "What about when you found out you let Reed Kincaid, your husband's friend and partner, in your pants? You're bound to see him again sometime."

Trust Vickie to speak with embarrassing bluntness. Heat stole over Lily's face again, but she answered with straightforward honesty. "I was thrilled someone wanted *me*, not a stranger. I'd forgotten that simple joy."

"I'm sorry, Lily. I hope you realize the fault is John's, not yours."

Empathy colored her friend's voice. Vickie, like Levi, meant well and always had her best interests at heart. One of the perks of family. "I do, I only wish it hadn't taken me so long."

"Okay, back to that hunk, Reed. Now you have his identity, but did you remember the rumors about the Kincaids' private parties? The night Levi and I went to Casey's with you and John, we did our share of speculating."

"I remember that night, but need I remind you about believing everything you hear? Besides, his sexual proclivities don't matter. We don't run in the same circles anymore, which makes it unlikely we'll see each other again." *You ever need anything, call me.* Those simple words kept popping up since Reed whispered them at John's wake, the first time she'd heard them from a man other than her brother. She figured that explained the comfort they offered during her down moments. Shoving that inane thought aside, Lily said, "Which is good because, as much as I relished every touch and spark, I'm not sure I can handle such intensity again."

Vickie raised her brows. "I don't hear you denying his dominance turned you on, but we can move on and discuss this mugger. What happened?"

Recalling her response to Reed's controlling hold sent tiny ripples of pleasure ghosting across her skin, the same feedback she'd experienced all week.

She welcomed the diversion of changing the subject. To hide the lingering unease from that fright, she shifted her gaze to the weed-infested gardens and dandelion-strewn yard before answering.

"He came running from, I assume, the unlit backside of the building, masked and cloaked as a demon, or something spooky. I didn't see much other than the bat he swung at me." She flipped Vickie a quick grin. "I ducked fast, the way Levi taught me."

Vickie frowned instead of returning her smile. "A mugger wielding a bat? Sounds more like a deliberate assault, someone out to hurt someone else."

Lily shook her head. "Maybe, but doubtful he targeted me. I didn't keep in touch with anyone around here except Trina while gone, and, other than you two and clients, I've only touched base with Delia at the pharmacy since I returned. Besides, no one has a reason to come after me like that, and the police agreed it was likely a random incident. I've put it behind me already."

Vickie cast her a dubious glance that turned decisive as she stood up. "We're going out tonight and kicking up our heels. Your fall off your saintly pedestal calls for celebrating. I vote for Casey's."

Lily jerked and jumped up. "Wait a minute!

That's the club the Kincaids own."

"Yes, but Reed isn't aware you've discovered his identity, right?"

"I don't see how, but talk about awkward, if he's there." Her pulse went haywire at the possibility of seeing him again, and she wouldn't mind checking his reception to coming face-to-face with her again, but questioned her own reaction to seeing him. Her acting skills were nil.

"You've already proven you can handle yourself. Don't go all wimpy on me now. Come on. Let's raid your closet. A shopping trip might be in order before we leave."

Lily's phone rang as they got into her SUV, and she sighed, not wanting to talk to Delia, preferring to hang out with just Vickie tonight. She let the call go to voice mail and dropped her cell back into her purse.

"Who are you avoiding?" Vickie asked, settling on the passenger seat.

"Delia. I'll call her tomorrow. Remember, you agreed to leave when I'm ready, regardless of how long we've been there." She kept bouncing back and forth between looking forward to seeing Reed and fretting over what he might say. Would he come clean about his identity last week, or act as if this was their first encounter since she had returned from Florida? She couldn't decide which reaction she would prefer.

"No problem, Lil," Vickie assured her. "If nothing else, it will put an end to living with anxious speculation over your inevitable reunion. Eagle's Nest is much closer to the Kincaid ranch than Casper." She flicked Lily quick, sly, glance. "Maybe, subconsciously, that's why you bought a place in the small suburb. Anyway, you mentioned his brother and fiancée signed on with Creative Events for their wedding. There's no way around not running into Reed again at some point. May as well get it over with."

Lily's memory lapse about that fact proved she still needed to come to terms with her behavior last weekend. "Sometimes I dislike it when you add a dose of common sense into the equation, but I'll have you know, I wasn't thinking about Reed Kincaid a few weeks ago when I bought the house. I like the big yard."

"You always did enjoy tending your gardens, and we benefitted when you shared the produce."

They reached the highway, the headlights cutting through the dark, both of them keeping an eye out for potential deer crossings while Lily tried not to second-guess her decision to go to Casey's. Vickie was right; she would lose sleep over running into Reed again.

"I am planning a garden, but I also want a dog. John didn't care for pets."

"I get spoiling privileges."

"Sure," she replied as she pulled into the crowded parking lot in front of the renovated roadside club.

Strolling to the well-lit door, Vickie pointed toward the end of the building. "I never could talk Levi into visiting their playroom upstairs, even though he still threatens to haul me up there when I get bitchy."

"John didn't share Reed's interest in that lifestyle but told me all about it. He went as a guest one night before we met and admitted watching was a turn-on. But then, he found women in general a turn-on."

Opening the door, Vickie replied, "At least now you can admit his faults with a touch of humor. That's progress. Let's go achieve some more progress."

Lily didn't recognize the country western tune resonating with the laughter and loud voices spilling from the cavernous room as they entered. The vacant tables were few, but they weaved through the throng until they found one in between the center dance floor and mechanical bull in the far corner. Everything appeared the same as the last time she and John were here, over two years ago. Between bodies, she caught a glimpse of Jordon Myers, the club manager, manning the bar, but so far, no other familiar faces. That didn't stop her from rubbing her clammy hands down the sides of her denim skirt before sitting down.

"Save our seats while I get drinks, okay?" Vickie asked, leaning down to talk over the noise level.

Nodding, she mouthed, "Rum and Coke."

With a thumbs-up, Vickie disappeared into the crowd, leaving Lily alone. The club scene had never appealed to her, not even in her younger days before marrying. She'd spent enough weekends clubbing and dancing during college to last her a lifetime. Now she preferred quieter places and entertainment, like eating pizza and popcorn while watching a mystery movie. Then again, the man approaching her with an engaging smile could change her mind. Tall and lean, his wavy brown hair slid forward across his brow as he braced his hands on the table.

"Care to dance, darlin'?"

An ego-boosting feminine thrill shot through

her, close but with less intensity than she'd felt when Reed found her on the patio last week. Lily only allowed herself one second of hesitation before nodding, determined to have fun tonight.

Taking his hand, she went up on her toes to tell him, "It's been ages since I've danced like that. Are you sure?" She hoped the two-step moves would come back to her as easy as riding a bike again.

"I'm a damn good teacher, so yes, I'm sure. I'm Matt." He tugged her onto the dance floor, stopping at the edge of the gyrating patrons instead of squeezing into the middle of them.

"Lily," she said, grateful for his insight.

Without a lot of people bumping into them, she followed his lead and fell into the rhythm with no problem. Her tense muscles loosened, and her misgivings about coming out tonight were forgotten as she focused on not making a fool of herself. Her breathing grew labored by the end of the second song, and she planned to call it quits, but a slow ballad started next, and Matt pulled her into his arms.

Lily shuddered, the closer contact reminding her of Reed's firmer hold, his taller, broader body pressing against her, the memory so vivid it could have happened yesterday instead of last week.

"Relax." Matt smiled with reassurance. "No pressure for anything except a dance."

She tried and leaned into him, just getting comfortable with the contact when she looked over his shoulder and spotted Reed at the door. An electric jolt went through her, her blood warming seeing his gaze zeroed in on her. Even from halfway across the spacious, crowded room, she could detect the tight set to his jaw.

"You okay?" Matt asked, concern reflected in his tone.

He seemed so nice and attentive, she asked herself why she now preferred Reed's company. "Sorry. I saw someone I haven't seen in a while is all." *One week.* Before she could gather her wits, Reed came toward her, and she held her breath, wondering what he intended to do and say.

Reed wasn't prepared to see Lily at Casey's tonight, but his eyes were drawn like magnets toward the dancers. He would notice that long, mahogany braid anywhere. He paused a moment, adjusting to the surge of heat rushing through his veins at this unforeseen curveball. His heart pounding in reaction, he watched her laugh, her skirt flaring around her calves with her fast, two-stepping moves, her face suffused with pleasure then turning uncertain as the music slowed to a ballad and her partner pulled her closer. Recalling with a stab of jealousy the press of those soft curves against his body and her whispered pleas propelled him forward.

He hoped Matt Wilson wouldn't take affront as he placed a hand on his neighbor and friend's shoulder and asked, "Mind if I cut in? I haven't seen Lily in a while."

Matt's face remained neutral as he replied, "It's up to Lily."

She laid a hand on Matt's arm, face turning pink. It's fine. I...I'd like to catch up with Reed. Like he said, it's been a while."

"Thanks. I owe you." Reed slapped him on the shoulder in appreciation, and Matt dipped his head.

"Yes, you do. Catch you some other time, Lily."

"Thanks for the dance." She shifted her gaze up to Reed, frowning as he took his friend's place. "I planned to say hello if I saw you tonight. How've you been?"

Neither her look nor tone hinted she knew he was the one disguised as Don Juan last week, which settled the question of whether or not to come clean about his identity right away. Decency dictated he would explain sometime soon, but, right now, he couldn't bear to say anything sure to push her away before they got properly reacquainted.

"Good. You? How was your trip away?"

Reed wrapped an arm around her waist, his gaze traveling over her face and down her arched neck, enjoying her soft curves pressed close again way too much. The low cut of her white, sleeveless silk top revealed the top swell of her breasts, his fingers itching to toy with her responsive nipples, tug on them until they hardened into bumpy pinpoints.

Her words pushed his lust aside. "It helped. The guilt, I mean."

He swayed with her, moving their clasped hands up and down as they turned. "None of it was your fault, Lily. Remember, I left him, too, and he deserved us walking out of his life, especially you."

Lily nodded, the top of her head brushing his chin. "That I don't regret, only the time it took me to come to my senses. But I still believe his death makes no sense. He wasn't a careless drinker, and he fought taking prescriptions when they were necessary, so why would he mix the two?"

Her misgivings mirrored Reed's own, but the coroner's report left them no other explanation or reason for the cops to investigate further. She went on, "Still, there are a myriad of different ways for accidents like that to happen. And when I last checked, no one had found who may have been there with him for a while." According to friends at the police department, the woman who had joined John sometime the night before in giving his bed a workout had never come forward and there were no clues to her identity.

"Trust me, you have nothing to feel guilty about." To change the subject, he didn't let on he knew she'd returned and was working again at Creative Events when he asked, "When did you get back?"

She stiffened, releasing her pent-up breath before answering, "Almost five weeks ago. I planned to get in touch with you soon."

"I'm glad. I'd like to hear about your trip."

Lily turned the tables on him when she looked him square in the eye and said, "I expected you and your brothers to attend the benefit last weekend. The Kincaids always support the homeless shelter and food kitchens."

Reed couldn't tell if she was fishing, but it didn't matter. He refused to lie to her. The ballad ended and the tempo of the music picked up again. Leaning down, he put his lips to her ear. "Let's walk outside where it's quiet."

She paused, and he turned his head as she went on her toes to reply. Reed almost groaned when she spoke against his mouth, holding her even closer when she quivered, saying, "I'm with Vickie."

Taking her hand, he led her off the dance floor, scanning the tables until he spotted Vickie, whom he'd met only once. As luck would have it, Allie saw them before he got to Lily's table, waylaying them with a beaming smile.

"We finally made it. Are you headed to the bar?" She turned to Lily, holding out her hand. "Hi. I'm Allie, this guy's soon-to-be sister-in-law."

Lily took her hand. "Lily Regan. I believe you've booked your wedding with Creative Events, where I work. Nice to meet you, but I have to get back to my friend." She pointed to Vickie who waved.

"Lily. That's a pretty name." Allie flicked Reed a curious glance, and he shook his head, hoping she took the hint to keep quiet. His patience came close to snapping when Allie asked Lily, "Brett won't mind if we visit for a bit. I'd love to get your wedding ideas. Reed, will you get my drink from Brett?"

Not fooled by the innocent act, he gave Allie a curt nod. "Sure. Lily, thanks for the dance. We'll talk later."

Reed stalked toward the bar, and Lily could tell he wasn't happy about Allie's interference. She stood there eyeing his broad shoulders, the flash of his smile when he paused to speak with a patron, and questioned where the longing for his return was coming from. Tiny ripples still coursed through her body from their close embrace dancing, the warm sensation flowing through her veins a result of his deep voice in her ear. She experienced those same responses last week when he had his hands on her breasts, his fingers moving inside her.

Maybe I'm just horny.

Allie's giggle drew her attention. Had she spoken aloud? "All three Kincaids have that effect on women. I'm sorry. My timing sucked, didn't it?"

"A little but it's fine." Reed intended to speak with her again, and she guessed he would admit to his costumed performance. Lily could use the wait to get herself under control before dealing with him and that disclosure. "Let's sit down."

They joined Vickie who didn't waste a minute before teasing Lily. "Thanks for that entertainment, Lil. Please tell me you two made plans to further your reunion." She punctuated her comment by wiggling her eyebrows.

"As a matter of fact, he wants to talk later." Lily

introduced Allie then quickly changed the subject. "I'm looking forward to working on your wedding. I've seen the plans in place already and have a few ideas to pass on at your next appointment."

Allie smirked then told Vickie, "She changed the subject."

"She's good at that." Vickie swallowed the last of her drink and lifted the empty glass. "Time for another. You good since you're just starting?" she asked Lily.

"Yes, thanks."

As soon as Vickie left, Allie turned serious. "Reed's a good guy. If you're at all interested, you should give him a chance."

While she appreciated the honesty, Lily wasn't sure what she wanted from Reed, if anything. No, that wasn't true. No sense in denying the obvious. She seemed to desire what he could do to her that she'd never experienced with anyone else. When she thought of the risks she'd taken last week – engaging in a tryst with a stranger in such a public place while still on the job – instead of her actions causing worry, she quivered with an unexplained need. Before that night, sex was straight vanilla, and enjoyable, or so she'd thought.

"I'm well aware he is seen as a good catch, but

I'm not long out of a bad marriage and don't want to make another mistake. My husband told me all about their private parties, and I'm not into all that. He's a friend."

"Friends don't dance like that, and how do you know until you explore the possibilities? I once believed that, too. Want to see the upstairs where they get together?"

"*Oooh*, I do." Vickie arrived in time to hear the offer. "Come on, Lil, let's get adventurous. We'll look around, fantasize, and that'll be the end of it. It will give me something to tease Levi about when he goads me."

Temptation tugged at Lily, surprising her. Was it her interest in Reed or what goes on up there pushing her to say yes?

"You're hesitating, thinking too much. I started by touring the space. Brett convinced me to give it a try." Allie stood. "Grab your drinks, ladies, and let's go. We'll stop at the bar and get permission and my drink from Brett."

What the heck, Lily mused, following the other women. What did she have to lose? If nothing else, maybe it would pique her imagination enough to replace her fearful dreams about the attack with erotic fantasies she'd never contemplated before.

Funny how the two unexpected encounters after the charity fundraiser last week were the best and worst happenings that had occurred in her life the past few years.

Reed was nowhere around when they stopped at the bar, but Brett agreed to let Allie give them a tour upstairs since the space wasn't in use. That made taking the outside stairs up to the second floor much easier, but the first thing Lily did upon eyeing the apparatus along one wall was take a big gulp of her drink. Tremors rippled through her body as Allie described three different benches, one designed to prop a woman on elbows and knees doggie style.

Nope, no way, no how, she thought until she pictured Reed standing behind her, his rough hands on her bared body. A surge of volcanic heat chased away the tremors, leaving her to question her sanity.

"I'm pretty adventurous, but not this daring," Vickie commented when they walked down the short hall and peeked in a window to view what looked like a gynecologist's table.

"Brett and I have played in here, but with the shades closed. There are a few members who don't mind that much exposure in public. Over here is an office, and I'm still amazed at the Doms' creativity. It's always entertaining if you're not the one in a punishment scene."

Lily laughed at Allie's wince. "Spoken with experience?"

"Just once," she muttered then pointed to the last door. "A private bedroom." She drew them back toward the main area that resembled a lodge gathering space with its large seating areas around a floor-to-ceiling stone fireplace and corner bar if you could ignore the bondage equipment. "Putting the kink aside, the parties are fun, the members a great bunch of people I've enjoyed getting to know. Ready?"

They nodded and started toward the door when it opened and Reed entered with Brett, his laser gaze pinning Lily in place as images of the two of them alone up here flitted through her head. She shivered, a burning awareness of some deep, previously unknown need coursing through her, lit last week by his mere presence then his touch, now stoked into a crackling heat. He must have read something of her confusion and yearning on her face because he didn't pause long before striding forward with a determined glint in those sometimes too observant gray-green eyes.

"Allie, Vickie, if you don't mind giving me a few minutes alone with Lily." His commanding tone made it clear he wasn't requesting.

That didn't stop Vickie from glancing at Lily, asking, "Shall I wait downstairs for you?"

"Yes, thanks. This won't take long." She figured Reed wanted to clear the air between them. That worked for her. Then she could get past this consistent wondering if her response to him was a one-time thing she would eventually get over or a stronger pull toward something brewing that was both exciting and a touch scary.

"If that's the case, too bad," Allie quipped with a teasing grin.

"Allie," Brett growled.

"Coming."

Lily got a kick out of those two, but her humor fled as soon as the door closed behind them, leaving her alone in this room filled with decadent fantasies and Reed's large presence.

Chapter Six

When Reed returned inside Casey's after helping their bouncer Eric evict a disorderly patron and Brett told him Lily was getting a tour upstairs, his leaping pulse nearly jumped through his skin. Brett, the jerk, laughed. Jordon's curiosity shone in his eyes.

Slapping him on the shoulder, his brother stated, "Come on. Let's go up and get them."

Returning and striding up the stairs, his thoughts centered not on getting her out of there but binding her to an apparatus. The persistent pipe dream of tying her to him popped up on the direct heels of fantasizing a long session tormenting her delectable body and savoring her responses. That ongoing craving had lessened before seeing her again but never subsided all the way. Taking a fortifying breath before entering the upper private floor, he went inside. One look at her face confirmed what he started to suspect when he first took her in his arms downstairs, and his determination to apologize and let her go crumbled like a ton of bricks.

The cavernous space echoed with the shut of the door behind the girls and Brett, and Reed braced to do what he must. Marching over to Lily, he fisted his hands on his hips to keep from touching her again. Holding her close on the dance floor had been enough torture for one night.

"You figured out it was me in costume," he stated, getting right to the point.

She didn't appear mad or upset when she dipped her head. "Yes, but not until you walked away and stepped under the light, removing your wig and mask. Great disguise."

Her soft lips tilted upward at the corners, signaling her acceptance without passing negative judgment – for now anyway. The easing of his conscience went a long way toward leaving him open to other possibilities, like maybe she wasn't still as mired in her negative past relationship as he'd believed.

Relying on honesty was always the best policy, he replied, "I started to tell you who I was when I saw you in the welcoming line, but then you stopped me, and I let you." No excuses there. "Seeing you outside caught me by surprise. I thought you were in the back somewhere or already left, and when I noticed you were upset, I could only think of one thing. To help in any way I could. Did I choose the wrong way?"

With only a slight hesitation, Lily placed her hand on his bare forearm, the light touch seeping into his skin, her golden-brown eyes darkening. "I'll be just as open and honest. No. Besides, being who, or"—she glanced around the room—"I should say, what you are was exactly what I needed. At the time."

The quick way she added those last three words amused Reed but also prompted him to question whether they were true or not. They were alone now and talking with open candor. A perfect combination to test the waters it appeared they were both wading through, albeit, likely for different reasons. For her, he would guess a slight interest on her part for more of those climaxes that released hidden inhibitions and need. His only longing had always been for her.

"Are you sure?" Clasping her hand, Reed dared taking another chance on her and tugged Lily toward a single chain dangling from the ceiling and shorter one at the bottom of the wall. He gave her a second to eye the cuffs on the end of each then asked, "Lily, do you trust me?"

"Yes, of course." Her reply burst out as fast as

her denial seconds ago.

"That's key. Brett, Allie, Vickie, and Jordon all know we're up here, so answer me this. Do you trust *me*, not last weekend's stranger in disguise, enough to give a short bondage scene a try?"

Lily glanced at the chains again, not with indecision but curiosity. The tiny pulse in her neck picked up speed as she slid her eyes back up to him, jerking her head in agreement.

"I need the words, Lily." He couldn't afford any misunderstandings between them.

"Yes, I trust *you* enough. As weird as it sounds to me, I can't imagine doing this with anyone else right now. Maybe because you already broke the ice last time or because I know you, at least better than anyone else who does"—she waved an arm around the room—"this."

"Odds are, your interest, for whatever reason, has been there since you first heard aspects about the lifestyle from my relationship with John. Kick off your shoes," he instructed, moving forward without delay before one or both of them decided this wasn't a good idea.

As she toed off the blue pumps, he lifted her right hand and wrapped the cuff around her wrist. She dropped onto her bare feet, sucking in an audible gasp from the tighter stretch then tugging on her raised arm, face flushing. Reed drew further encouragement from watching her nipples peak under the thin silk and reached out to graze one finger across a puckered nub.

"Your body is speaking for you, but, again, I need your words, Lily." He started to say "sweetheart," but she'd heard endearments all too often from John, who tossed them out to all women with a frequency that lacked any real emotion behind them. She'd heard *just words* enough.

"I wasn't prepared for the…I'm not sure how to describe it. Sorry."

"Don't be. That's the honesty I want," he returned, pleased. Squatting down, he attached the lower cuff around her ankle, the scant three-inch chain keeping her close to the wall and restricting the movement of that leg. Rising, he cupped her face, holding her head tilted back. "Say red if you want me to stop." Keeping his gaze pinned to hers, he slid one hand around to hold her nape under the long braid, the other to mold one soft breast in his palm.

Lily trembled, the slight arch forward of her chest instead of shying away another sign of acceptance. Like last week, her quick responses amazed Reed, confirming how little he really knew about her. Or, maybe it was as simple as her not realizing what she could have had for years if she hadn't focused so long on saving a doomed relationship with a man she was once deeply in love with. He suspected that profound emotion had been dead long before she'd come to terms with the loss.

"What now? I mean...what are you going to do?"

Slight confusion and a wealth of longing colored her voice. *Perfect.* Reed released her breast to toy with the thin strap over her unbound shoulder. "Touch you while you get used to limited movement options. It will give you an idea of what full restraint will entail and whether or not you want to go that far next time."

Her eyes widened. "You're planning a next time?"

"Not yet. That's up to you. Later." He lowered the strap to her elbow, stopping short of allowing the thin scooped-neck top to drop far enough to reveal more than the lace edge of her bra. "Yes or no?"

Yes or no. How simple Reed made it sound, Lily mused, her body already primed for his bare touch. Her struggle wasn't near as much with the new sexual exploration but with whom she was indulging herself. How had she gone from always thinking of this man as nothing more than her husband's good-looking, nice friend and partner to pining for his sexual attention for a week? She wanted to blame it on sex and male attention deprivation but forced herself to admit there were no fantasies of getting close enough to anyone else to brave this.

Which made her answer easy.

"Yes."

Reed's slow smile of approval curled her toes. She could get used to that look, something to ponder later, when he wasn't exposing her left, demi-bra-covered breast and running a finger inside the cup. Tingles raced across her skin as he tugged the bra down, both breasts popping loose, the cool air caressing her sensitive flesh on the left, his rough hand kneading the fullness on the right. The odd combo of soft and hard, cool and warm sensations kept her mind and senses engaged, leaving no room for doubts to sneak in and ruin everything.

"So delicate, pretty, your nipples so fucking responsive. Let's test your threshold, and remember, red."

He didn't allow time for an answer before applying slow pressure to the nub, his gaze never wavering from her face. Lily trembled under his probing stare as he tightened his thumb and forefinger, grateful for his continued hold on her nape and the cuffs that enabled her to continue.

"*Oh,*" she breathed when her nipple went numb yet tiny pinpricks of pain stabbed all around the areola.

"God, I love your expressions."

Reed dipped his head and licked the tip of her aching nipple, setting off sparks. He covered her mouth next, his kiss hard and demanding as he slanted her head and released his fingers. Blood rushed to the tortured tip with a burst of hot agony, Lily's automatic reaction to escape meeting the resistance of her bound limbs. She groaned, but instead of wrenching her mouth free to speak, she opened for the slow, teasing exploration of his tongue. The discomfort disappeared as fast as it arrived, the warm throbbing that ensued more than pleasant, she discovered, when her pussy fluttered. Her chest heaving, she quivered as he pulled away and dropped both hands to her hips, his fingers playing with the side zipper on her skirt.

"Tell me green to keep going or red to stop. Keep in mind Vickie is waiting for you, and time is running short."

Lily loved the way he voiced her options with

few words and choices, leaving her little room or time to fret over making the right decision or question what the heck she was doing here, like this, with him again. She didn't delay, craving what he would deliver.

"Green."

Lowering the zipper, he replied, "Then give me a second to grab something to move you along before you're subjected to an audience."

Lily hadn't considered the impact of someone walking in on them, flushing at the thought, her skirt falling to her feet as Reed stepped over to a wall cabinet. The package he picked up gave her something else to think about, something that elicited a delicate shiver down her spine and sent her blood rushing heatedly through her veins. He returned to her side, ripping it open and holding up a short vibrator.

"Three speeds I'm told pack a quick wallop. Let's see. You can keep it if you like it." Clamping a hand on her hip, he nudged her panties far enough down to place the narrow, rounded end right between her pussy lips then flashed her a wicked grin that melted her heart. "Deep breath, Lily."

That was all she managed before the intense vibrations against her clit sent her into a climatic orbit of spiraling pleasure, her whole body jerking against the chain restraints and his grip, her free hand latching onto his thick forearm. She held tight, riding the waves of ecstasy, her inability to thrust and arch along with the tide of pleasure flowing through her body enhancing the euphoria to yet another level higher than she'd ever achieved before. Reed's low, soothing voice seeped into her head but she couldn't make out the words, not that they mattered.

Lily didn't return to full awareness until her clothes were righted, the cuffs removed, and she sagged against Reed. She sighed, trying to recall something that had felt better than his arms wrapping around her at that moment but couldn't think of a thing. They stood that way in silence except for her labored breathing, his chin resting on her head, until the door opened, drawing them apart.

Brett popped his head in and drawled, "Vickie asked me to confirm you're okay, but I see you are."

He started to close the door, but Reed stopped him. "We're headed down now."

"I'll let her know."

Reed took her hand, pausing a moment to subject her to one of those probing stares before he asked with a straightforwardness she appreciated,

"Between last week and tonight, I've put you through a lot. Are we good, Lily?"

"Yes, Reed, we're fine. Well, I am and hope you are." She now needed time to figure out what this all meant, what *he* meant to her.

"I told you last year I would be here for you, and that hasn't changed and won't change." He led her to the door, his fingers running over the bruise on her shoulder from her mugger's bat. "What happened here?"

His light touch kept her from pondering what he meant by that previous remark. "I ran into something, not paying attention. It's almost gone." She hoped he wouldn't question her further. She was having enough trouble looking away from his sharpened gaze to come up with anything else. The last thing she wanted to do was end the night talking about the attack she was trying to put behind her.

Reed's jaw tightened, but all he said was, "Be careful. You have delicate skin."

Vickie was waiting by the car as they descended the stairs, talking to someone who looked familiar, but Lily couldn't put a name to her face until Reed greeted her.

"Hey, Bianca. Did you ever meet Lily?"

The brunette smiled. "We met a few years back.

I just got here and recognized Vickie. How have you been, Lily?"

"Good, thanks. You're with the manager, Jordon, right?" She remembered seeing Bianca behind the bar with Casey's manager.

"We're still tight." Bianca sent Reed a teasing grin. "It takes too long to break these guys in to trade them in too often."

"Funny," Reed returned, opening the door then addressing Vickie. "You should drive."

"I was about to suggest that," Vickie said, catching the keys Lily tossed her despite the stab of annoyance with Reed for not asking her first.

Lily was tired and still trembling from Reed's attention, so she let it go. She couldn't think straight until she was away from him – he was just too distracting in more ways than one.

"Nice to see you again, Bianca." Turning to Reed, all she could think to say was, "Thank you."

"Good night, Lily, Vickie. Come back soon."

Lily's breathing seemed to calm once they pulled onto the highway and were heading home. She'd aways thought no man could muddle her thinking the way John did, but that was one more thing she'd been wrong about when it came to her husband.

"Do I get the salacious details, or would you rather keep them to yourself?" Vickie asked.

"Well, if you double what I told you about last week, you'll get a good idea."

"Cool." They both laughed then Vickie asked a harder question. "Are you going to see him again, give this a chance?"

"A chance at what, Vic? I'm not interested in another relationship, and, no, it's not because I'm still stupid enough to pine for John, or even mourn him. He would have to be a hell of a guy for me to commit to anyone again." She was an all-or-nothing woman, had her convictions and stuck by them. Her nature was to think of others first, do for them whenever she could, but in regard to getting involved again, risking her heart, she couldn't afford to make another mistake.

"I understand," Vickie said, turning into Lily's driveway. "But don't be so cautious you miss out on a good one. If nothing else, enjoy a sordid affair. God knows, you're overdue."

If the orgasms Reed had gifted her with were any sign, Vickie was right, and Lily was way overdue in that department. She couldn't imagine, though, letting anyone else do those things, trusting anyone else with her physical well-being the way she'd put herself in Reed's hands. Being with him tugged at more inside her than lust, and that required careful scrutiny before seeing him again.

"*Mmm*, I'll give that some thought," she said, stepping out of the car. As they strode toward the porch, screeching tires drew their attention down the street where Lily caught the taillights of a vehicle whipping around the corner. "I'll bet that's the teenager who just got his license. If he keeps that up, he'll get his first ticket in no time."

"Yeah, but at that age, it's worth a lecture from Mom and Dad to have fun with your first car." Vickie glanced at the dark porch, saying, "Didn't we leave the light on when we left?"

Lily frowned, pulling out her key. "I thought I did. Maybe I missed the switch." She glanced around the yard and then the porch, still uneasy at night even though Eagle's Nest was a safe community and the neighbors watched out for each other. "That wasn't it," she said as they went inside and she felt for the wall switch and found it on. "Must be a burned-out bulb."

"We can change it tomorrow, but I know we left that lamp on in the corner." Vickie's annoyed voice sounded loud in the dark.

Using her cell phone light, Lily found the

corner lamp, but it didn't light up when she turned the switch. "Okay, must be in the breaker box. Come with me. I can never figure these things out."

"This is why I don't like old houses," Vickie said at her side as they walked through the kitchen to the utility room with only their phone lights to guide them. "No amount of charm is worth all the things that can go wrong."

Chuckling despite the shakes from the dark, Lily bumped her with her elbow. "Lights can go out in any house. Make sure I do this right. Levi only showed me once." She opened the box and flipped the switches, and not only did the light in the other room come on, the whole house lit up.

"What the hell?" Vickie went down the hall then came back, shaking her head. "You're lit up like a Christmas tree, every single light, even the closets. You should call an electrician first thing Monday."

Lily released her breath, relief easing her tenseness with the bright illumination regardless of the electrical expense she was likely facing. She hoped entering a dark room or stepping outside at night wouldn't always cause her several moments of trepidation. "I will, but I can use a glass of wine before turning in."

"I'll join you."

The next morning, Lily saw Vickie off, promising to make a trip up to Cheyenne when Levi returned from his latest assignment. With Vickie gone, her thoughts shifted to Reed, and Vickie's suggestion to indulge in an affair. If she believed for one second she could spend a few weeks with Reed, or any man she found desirable and likable without engaging feelings, she might consider the idea. Her brother often took credit for her old-fashioned views regarding who and when she would sleep with a man, and she could now admit she appreciated his guidance and lectures during her teens.

If Levi only knew what I did the last two Saturday nights. He would lecture her until she was blue in the face, as only a protective big brother could. If he ever found out, she mused while cleaning up the kitchen, those encounters were worth listening to one of his sermons. She'd never been tempted to sleep with a man she didn't harbor deep feelings for, which gave her pause in considering anything more with Reed. Regardless that her shattered heart had healed a long time ago and she was well over John and the end of their marriage, she would not allow room to repeat her past mistakes.

Reed is different.

"Oh, shut up," Lily muttered, checking the

clock. She was scheduled to help at the shelter this morning and didn't have time to psychoanalyze herself or her actions. Which was good, because she had no idea where to begin when she thought about Reed now.

She remembered Delia's call last night as she arrived at the homeless shelter, and a stab of guilt for ignoring it poked her abdomen. Thinking of the busy work week ahead, she decided today would be best to make it up to her. If she could meet her at the farmer's market this afternoon, which only opened on weekends, they could get lunch there. If nothing else, the gesture would settle her conscience, Lily thought, pulling her phone out of her purse.

"Hey, Delia," Lily replied when she answered. "I saw you called last night."

"Oh, right. No big deal. I was going to see if you wanted to take in a movie or something. I went with a co-worker instead."

Lily felt much better hearing she hadn't sat around by herself all evening. "Good. If you don't have plans, I'm working at the shelter until around two today and then hitting the farmer's market. Want to meet me and grab a brat and corn on the cob?" The food truck that parked in the large downtown lot while the local farmers sold their produce and homemade goods did a booming business, their German brats the best Lily had ever tasted.

She paused before saying, "Sure, I'd like that. Haven't been by there in ages."

"I'll text you when I leave the shelter."

Lily reached into the back seat for the bags of clothing donations she'd picked up at Goodwill and entered the shelter, always saddened by the number of people in dire circumstances. Most of the homeless suffered from mental disorders, and the shelter's psychologist tried to counsel them, but they were the hardest people to help. Tables now replaced the cots set up for overnight stays, and she could smell lunch from the kitchen in the rear of the building as she paused on her way back to visit with a few regulars she'd gotten to know well.

Janie Lightfoot, a young widow with four-year-old twin boys, rushed up to her, holding a hand of each toddler and wearing a wide smile. "I got the job at the temp agency – thank you so much! It was your call that did it."

The little Janie and her husband had when he died last year had gone fast, and the small family ended up at the shelter during the holidays. Tears of gratitude shone in Janie's eyes, her lips trembling as she said, "We can move into the apartment in a few days, and I'll start paying you back for the deposit and first month's rent when I get paid. I'm so appreciative for your generosity."

They would be cramped in the studio apartment within walking distance of the bus stop until something larger opened up, but it got them off the street, and that's what mattered most right now. "Don't worry about paying me back. The daycare called for my reference, so I know the boys have been accepted for a year free. I'm happy for you."

Unfortunately, there weren't enough success stories, Lily thought, making her way to the kitchen. She handed the clothes to another volunteer then pushed through the swinging door to see Trina's teenage daughters filling buffet bins with food at the stoves.

"Hey, girls, good to see you helping out again."

"Hi, Ms. Regan," they chimed together without stopping their work.

"Gotta keep them out of trouble," Trina stated, turning from the oversized refrigerator with an armful of bagged salads. She halted and took a closer look that Lily tried to avoid. Padding over to her, a slow grin spread across Trina's face. "What did you do last night?"

Thank goodness she whispered the inquiry

so no one else in the kitchen heard. "Am I that obvious?" she asked, taking a few of the bags from her then striding to the end of the buffet.

"Tell me obvious about what, and I'll let you know."

Opening bags, they loaded the large salad bin as Lily pondered her answer then said, "I saw Reed again last night, and that's all I'm saying today."

Trina chuckled. "Enough said. You can give me details when we leave."

"I'm meeting Delia at the farmer's market, and I don't think your girls want to spend the rest of their day there." Now she was glad she'd made plans with Delia. She didn't want to discuss Reed with anyone else until she figured out why the man she hadn't given more than a fond passing thought to since meeting him all of sudden drew her like a magnet.

"No, and neither hesitated to come today, so I won't ask. Tomorrow, then. I didn't think you were chummy with your pharmacist."

Lily didn't know what had motivated Delia's interest in getting better acquainted since John died, but she liked her and sensed she could use a friend. She shrugged, picking up the tongs to toss the salad. "We're not, really. She's asked to hang out a few times, is all, and I have time today."

Trina patted her arm. "I've said it before, and likely will again. You're a nice person."

She thought of Pam, and her refusal to mend that fence. "Not always."

Working at the shelter could be a mental and physical strain some days, but with fewer people in need this week and Janie's job offer, today was not one of those days. Lily hung around a little longer than usual to help hand out the large intake of summer clothes dropped off over the past few weeks, sending Delia a text as she walked to her vehicle when she finished.

See you there, Delia returned and Lily spotted her easily enough by the food truck ten minutes later. It felt good being outside on such a sunny, warm afternoon, the slight breeze wafting across her skin reminding her of Reed's soft breath on her sensitive neck, his whisper against her lips. She sighed, wishing she could figure out why her reaction to him was so strong when other men just as appealing drew no response.

Delia greeted her with a speculative look. "Hi. Is something wrong?"

Lily cursed her expressive face. "No, why?"

"Your face is flushed, or the sun is getting to you already."

"The bane of fair skin, yet I love the outdoors during the warmer months. I'm starving. Ready to order?" She gestured toward the menu displayed on the side of the neon-blue truck as they got in the line to the serving window.

"I waited on lunch after you called. I guess the food at the shelter is gross, huh?" Delia wrinkled her nose.

"Not at all," Lily denied, thinking of the early morning hours the volunteer cooks put in, herself included sometimes. "We bake chicken tenders by the dozens, make hamburgers and gravy and mashed potatoes. The vegetables are canned and the salad bagged, but the proteins are fresh. But we never know how many will show up, and I don't want to take from anyone whose only decent meal is at the shelter."

Delia turned her back to Lily as they stepped up to the window, mumbling, "That's thoughtful."

She thought she heard a hint of snide derision in her tone, but Lily decided she must be mistaken. The parking lot for Casper's largest public park where the city held all its summer festivities was teeming with people loading up at the various booths of fresh produce and homemade condiments, making it hard to hear. They found a seat facing each other on the end of a picnic table and sat down.

"*Mmm*, I love these," Lily said around a mouthful of brat and German mustard.

"I've only been here once. It's easier to run into the store and pick up a frozen entrée for one when you live alone. But these are good."

That time, there was no mistaking the wistful sadness in Delia's voice, but Lily didn't know her well enough to pry into her personal life. She knew from experience there could be private, painful reasons for someone to stay to themselves. They chatted while they ate, watching people, nodding to those they recognized, and she found Delia as companionable as back when she'd joined her and Vickie for a movie. Vickie happened to be with her when Lily had stopped by the pharmacy to pick up a prescription, and Delia overheard them discussing what movie to watch that night. She'd extended the invitation out of courtesy after Delia mentioned an interest in the movie, never expecting her to pounce on accepting.

"Whoa, if looks could kill, one of us would be keeled over. Do you know her?"

Delia nodded to someone behind Lily, and she turned to catch Pam glaring at her from a booth several feet away before Pam spun around and stomped off. So much for her tearful remorse. Maybe she should at least make peace with her former best friend so these occasional run-ins weren't so tense.

"We were close in college but had a falling out about eighteen months ago," was all she told Delia.

"About the time you and John split? That must have been hard. I'm sorry." Lily's expression must have slipped because Delia's sympathetic gaze turned sharp, and she asked, "Oh, does your rift have to do with John?"

Lily nodded, hoping she would drop it. She didn't, and Lily had to call on her patience when Delia grimaced and said, "That sucks. Was that what made you finally leave? I don't date a lot – too picky, I guess – but I think I'd rather stay single and alone than go through what you did."

"Alone can be a lonely place after a while," Lily returned, a tad annoyed with her. "I've put all that behind me anyway. Ready? I want to get home before long to finish some chores." Rising, she pointed to a nearby booth. "They have the best corn on the cob and homemade jellies."

"Lead the way."

Lily was glad Delia smiled and didn't bring up her marriage again as they checked out the booths and filled their bags. If she could bring herself to smooth out her relationship with Pam, she would lay to rest the final chapter of that part of her life.

Chapter Seven

"He's pouting again."

Reed kept running the brush over Apollo's flank, ignoring Slade's comment to Brett as they dismounted their horses at the corral.

Brett looped the reins around the rail and nudged his hat up. "Now he's ignoring us."

"Because you're both annoying morons," he replied without looking away from his grooming. His free hand rested on Apollo's shoulder, the stallion's warm coat soft against his palm.

"It's been almost two weeks since you were with Lily upstairs at Casey's," Brett pointed out, sliding off Shadow's saddle.

Naturally, Slade wouldn't hesitate to jump on that even though he wasn't there. "And you've never hesitated to call someone you're interested in, so what are you waiting for?"

Leaning his forearms on the top rail, Slade pinned Reed with a direct stare as he shuffled to

Apollo's other side. "I don't pester you about never seeing anyone outside our small private group," he pointed out to Slade.

Slade flashed him a grin. "Because that's nothing new for me. You, on the other hand, are the outgoing, fun brother. Or, you used to be."

"Still am when my brothers aren't nagging me," he quipped, returning the grin. It required way too much effort to hold onto a snit with either of his siblings.

"Better us than Allie," Brett taunted.

Reed stiffened and aimed the brush at Brett. "You tell her to butt out, Brett. I mean it." He didn't want any more surprises with Lily.

Brett released Shadow into the pasture to follow Bandit. "All she said was we should invite her to the surprise birthday party you're pretending you know nothing about."

Laughing, Reed walked with them toward their trucks. "You invited all the hands. Did you expect them to keep quiet?"

"No, I didn't, but Mom believed they would go along with the surprise part," Slade replied.

"In their defense, the guys standing around jawing about it didn't see me in the stable, and, as far as I'm aware, they have no clue they spilled the beans unless either of you mentioned it. But I'm still good at playing innocent with Mom."

"Like when I chased you through the house and you knocked over the Christmas tree and blamed me?" Brett shot back.

"I wouldn't have been grabbing for it coming around the corner if you weren't hell-bent on plowing into me," he returned without remorse for the days Brett spent grounded over the holiday.

"*Ah*, good times," Slade drawled. "Ask Lily out tonight. It'll make it easier for her to say yes when Allie talks Mom into inviting her to your party."

"Damn it!" Reed flung the curse at Brett when they paused in front of the stable. "Don't let her say a word to Mom."

"I'll talk to her. Seriously. But why not take out Lily? You can always pretend it's as a friend, or a follow-up on how she's doing since you saw her last. Slade and I assume you weren't talking that whole time."

Removing his hat, Reed raked his fingers through his hair, pushing it off his damp forehead before replacing his Stetson, ignoring the speculation etched on his brothers' faces. Other than the occasional play parties they hosted where their involvement with women was often depicted in a public scene, they kept their private lives private. After growing up with a philandering father who didn't know the meaning of discretion, they vowed never to give the tabloids the same ammo to publicize. But Brett made a good point. He should check back with Lily. Despite ensuring her stability before escorting her downstairs again, he should have at least called her the next day. The last thing he wanted was for her to regret anything they had done so far.

"No, we weren't just talking, but don't push for more. She hasn't shown an interest in me other than as a friend, except for that night, and then her interest was in the relief she experienced from that introduction, not in me." And he'd spent way too much time since the charity benefit wishing otherwise. What had occurred there would stay between them unless Lily chose to tell someone else. "I will stop by, though, since your suggestion to follow up with her is something I should have done a lot sooner."

Brett fisted his hands on his hips. "Don't beat yourself up over it, Reed. Lily has muddled your thinking for a few years. After what I went through with Allie, I can now not only understand but sympathize how one woman can tie you up knots that are fucking hard to loosen."

Slade shook his head. "Sounds to me it would be easier to not let those knots tighten in the first place."

"Easy for you to say when you haven't met the right one yet," Reed told him, taking a step toward his truck. His gaze shifted toward the barn, anger replacing his restored good mood when he saw the college hands come out of the barn, both Evan and Riley with lit cigarettes. "Those fucking shitheads! Put those damn things out, now!"

Slade dropped a hand on his shoulder and squeezed, preventing him from stalking over there and laying into the college kids for disobeying one of their most important safety rules. One small ember landing on dry hay inside any of the ranch buildings could set off an uncontrollable blaze within minutes.

Reed swung on Slade, knocking off his hand when Evan's face turned insolent as he crushed the cigarette under his boot. "Why the hell do you keep that little prick employed here? He's done nothing to get rid of the chip on his shoulder from day one."

Brett crooked a finger at all three hands while Slade said, "From what the others have let slip around me, Evan grew up without a father, his mother never hiding her bitterness over that affair.

We were lucky. Dad neglected his parental duties but loved us and was around. Plus, we benefitted from Ward's influence where Dad was lacking. I won't give up on the kid yet, on any of them."

Slade stomped toward the trio, meeting them halfway but far enough from Reed and Brett they couldn't make out what he was saying. From the fury of his arm gestures and the guys' pale, flinching expressions, his words and consequences were harsh. Good, Reed thought, getting into his truck. When their father had left Slade in charge of the hands and the ranch, he and Brett were still working their career choices, only too happy to leave the day-to-day running of the ranch in their little brother's capable hands. Though he had resigned from the highway patrol a while ago and Brett had cut his legal practice hours in half so they could work their inheritance full-time they remained content leaving the burdensome chore of employees with Slade.

Reed shut the door then leaned out the window. "See you tomorrow. Don't forget to talk to Allie, and keep her away from Mom for the next week."

"It's our turn to have Sunday dinner with her family this weekend, so you can discuss it with Mom on your own, but I'll warn her again to stay out of your business. One thing, Reed."

"What?"

"You were aware I wanted Allie in the first weeks of meeting her and asked me what I had to lose by giving her a chance. It's been close to four years since I saw your interest in Lily, so I'll ask you, what have you got to lose now?" Brett grinned and got into his truck, lifting his hand in a wave. "After you answer that question, tell her I said hello."

Reed drove to his house contemplating Brett's surety that he would go see Lily, prompting him to quit ignoring how much the idea appealed to him. As he showered, he went over the things he'd learned about Lily over the years – her compassion for those less fortunate, her determination to do what was right, whether it's something she wanted to do or not, her refusal to retaliate against John with an affair of her own or to leave until she was sure there was no hope he would change, her sweet disposition, and the spark of fire when she was pushed too far he'd only glimpsed once. He finished showering with a raging hard-on, his mind and body in agreement with how much he longed for Lily in his life, if only he could be sure she wanted him the same way.

Reed decided there was only one way to find out and thirty minutes later, he parked in front of Ina's to pick up the order he called in, hoping Lily hadn't eaten yet. He remembered John mentioning her favorite food was lasagna, which happened to be the Friday night special. If his idea to stop by without calling first would go in his favor, also, he wouldn't ask for much more than that.

Lily didn't live far from his mother's house, but, in Eagle's Nest, no one lived far from anyone else due to the small size of the town. The stately elm in her front yard spoke the age of the cozy bungalow where he found her kneeling in the garden bed to the left of the front porch. He had time to appreciate her soft butt in denim cutoffs before she stood and pivoted as he parked in the drive. Her jaw dropped in surprise then she pressed her lips together and removed her gardening gloves as he got out.

Leaning an arm on the open door, Reed stayed there as he said, "I hope you haven't eaten dinner yet."

"Why?" she asked, coming toward him.

The hint of caution in her voice was not unwelcoming, and neither was the pleasure that suffused her face when her gaze landed on the take-out bag from Ina's.

"Because I took a chance on you being home and hungry about now. Ina's special tonight is lasagna."

She looked up at him with a slow smile. "You remembered. Why didn't you call?"

"You know, Lily," he replied, reaching for the bag, "that's one of the things I like about you. When you're not flustered or distracted, or upset, you have no problem asking a straightforward question."

"Yes, well, the two times I've seen you since coming back home, I've been both flustered and distracted. You can settle my confusion tonight while we eat. Come in and give me a minute to wash up."

I'm not here for sex, Reed lectured himself when he followed Lily inside and his eyes were again drawn to her butt and legs. But, damn, she looked good in a pair of shorts. He was pleased with her reception, so now, all he had to do was stay focused on his goal of starting a relationship and not on getting her naked.

Lily waved a hand toward the kitchen as Reed shut the door behind him. "Have a seat, and I'll hurry."

"Take your time. It'll warm up if needed, and you weren't expecting me."

He subjected her to another potent, scrutinizing gaze that never failed to get her blood pumping faster, and guessed he was searching for a sign she objected to his surprise visit. She'd spent the last two weeks trying to come to terms with how much she wanted Reed after thinking of him as nothing more than a friend for so long. Now, he was here, in her house, and her only reaction to his sudden presence was a thrill of happiness.

"No, but it's not a problem. You had me at lasagna." He grinned at that and her heart did a little flip. "Be right back." Lily dashed into the bathroom and washed her hands and face, wishing she had time to put on a little makeup. Instead, she quickly redid her braid, which was coming out then used a light floral body spray while questions about his visit ran through her head. Gazing in the mirror, she muttered, "The only way for answers is to get back out there."

"You have quite the collection," Reed stated from where he now stood checking out her mystery movies and books on shelves next to the fireplace.

Lily padded over, proud of her alphabetical display. "It's taken years to amass all these. If a movie is made from a book, I like to read the book first then watch the video. Sometimes, though, the changes script writers make for the movie version are irritating."

Her stomach grumbled at that moment, and

Reed sent her an amused look, placing his hand on her lower back. Even through her top, Lily felt his touch all the way to her toes. She didn't fight the pleasure or question her response again. Why bother when she'd been unable to find answers for her attraction to him for what, several weeks now?

"Food's getting cold, and I'm as hungry as you sound. What do you have to drink?"

Glad he was making this easier with his casual dialogue, she replied, "Beer, tea, and water. Vickie and I finished my wine and I haven't replaced it yet."

"I'll have tea, and, next time, we can go out and have wine with dinner."

Lily went to the cabinet and retrieved two tall glasses, keeping her back to him for a moment so he wouldn't notice the quick zing of happiness she was sure reflected on her face. If he was already planning a next time, maybe tonight wasn't just a stop-by-and-check-on-her visit. She filled the glasses with ice and tea and set them on the table before grabbing silverware from a drawer.

"That smells awesome," she noted, taking a seat across from Reed where he had opened a take-out box containing a large portion of still-hot, cheese-smothered lasagna. She glanced at his order and grinned. "Meatloaf and potatoes. The men all seem to love that dish."

"What can I say? We're easy to please, not to mention the Hendersons always cook from scratch, like my mom. Nothing tastes better." He took a bite of potatoes then said, "This place looks good. Did it need a lot of repair work?"

She beamed at him, pleased he noticed all of her efforts. "Not too much. The inspection found a few things the seller agreed to fix, and there's only been a glitch with the electric since. Vickie and I returned from Casey's to no lights." She shuddered, remembering the pitch darkness that had resurrected her fear from the late-night mugging. She just now realized the strange coincidence that both incidents occurred after being with Reed.

Reed put down his glass, his gaze narrowing. "What? Did something happen?"

I have to stop forgetting how astute he is.

Lily didn't want to ruin the meal by bringing up the attack on her, so she hedged around it without lying. "I'm a wimp when it comes to dark places. I like mysteries, not scary or horror films." She concentrated on taking several bites and missed his displeasure until he spoke again.

"Lily, what happened? Did you have a break-in? Was someone lurking around the house?"

If he had her in restraints and used that tone, she was sure she wouldn't hesitate to give him a full accounting. There had been something about his authority and her vulnerability that had triggered a hidden need inside her she still couldn't define. Thankfully, there was a table between them and he wasn't muddling her thinking with his touch.

"No, nothing like that. We got spooked is all. The electrician showed me where several wires had become frayed." Reed eyed her as he ate the last bite of meatloaf, and Lily forced herself not to squirm under his intense regard, not relaxing until he changed the subject to a topic she was more than comfortable with.

"I saw the movie *Clue* on your shelves. Is it any good?"

"That's a recent purchase, and I haven't had time to watch it yet." She closed the lid on the box, saving the other half of her meal for tomorrow, hoping he didn't have to leave yet. It was nice not spending the evening alone. Or maybe it was his company she found so enjoyable. "As good as my lasagna is, there's no way I can finish it. Thank you. I owe you one."

"You can pay me back by inviting me to stay and watch the movie with you, if you don't have plans."

"I don't," she answered, excitement over the unexpected suggestion humming inside her.

"Point me to your outdoor trash, and I'll take this out while you put yours away." He put his empty container and napkins back in the bag as she nodded toward the door off the kitchen.

"Right outside that door. Thanks."

Lily found herself grateful for Reed's take-charge attitude, a trait she'd believed he reserved for when he was in Dom mode. He seemed to know she was still puzzling over his impromptu get-together. Padding to the refrigerator, she put her leftovers inside then went to get the movie ready. She was slipping it into the DVD player when he returned, his tall, broad-shouldered body seeming to shrink her small living room.

Taking a seat in the middle of the sofa, he held out his hand, her heart somersaulting as she took it and he tugged her down next to him. He put a booted foot on his other thigh, the bent knee lightly touching her leg below her shorts, the denim rough in a tingly way against her bare skin.

Tucking their clasped hands against the inside of his thigh, Reed stated, "Ready when you are."

"Oh, ready," Lily returned, flustered from the warm rush of blood flow through her veins. This could be the longest ninety minutes of her life if they stayed this close, his hand wrapped around hers through the whole show.

During the next hour and a half, Lily couldn't think of a time when she had enjoyed watching a movie with someone else more. Unless it was Vickie and/or Levi joining her, she preferred trying to solve the mysteries by herself. But Reed knew when to stay silent so they wouldn't miss a clue, and when to mention an observance, twice catching something she missed because she'd been more attuned to his nearness than on the show. When the credits rolled and he rose from the sofa, tugging her up with him, needy, lust-filled expectations caused her pulse to skip a beat.

"Good movie," Reed said, keeping hold of her hand as he headed to the door, squashing her hopes he would stay the night. "Thank you for letting me intrude on your evening and sharing it with me."

"I enjoyed it, and your company." At the door, Lily again questioned his motive behind this visit if he hadn't wanted more than a shared meal and movie.

"You're confused because I'm ending the evening without seducing you into another scene." Wrapping his free hand around her braid at her nape, he yanked, the tug on her scalp pulling her head back, her face upward. She opened her mouth, and he took advantage of her surprise to cover her lips, gifting her with one of his devastating kisses.

Unable to help herself, Lily moaned, leaning into him as he drew their clasped hands behind her to press against her lower back. She returned his kiss with enthusiasm, holding nothing back, welcoming his stroking tongue and following the slide of his mouth over hers. Her lips were throbbing when he released her, their heavy breathing the only sound for a moment.

"To answer the question in your eyes, this was about more than sex."

Her throat went dry. "How much more?"

"The start of a relationship. You're ready, and so am I." Reed picked up his hat from the small table next to the door and put it on then gave her a quick kiss. Opening the door, he said, "It's my turn to assist Jordon at Casey's tomorrow night, if you want to keep me company."

Excitement flitted inside Lily, causing her stomach to cramp and her heart to race despite her mind still processing how she felt about entering into another relationship. Her nerves quivered at the idea, yet she couldn't think of another man she had ever craved as much as Reed these past few weeks. Not even John, whom she had loved with her whole heart and tried so hard to hold on to.

Stepping onto the porch with him, she sucked in a deep breath. "I'll try." She didn't want to commit until she thought it through, not after she had fallen so fast for John and jumped at the chance to marry him way too soon.

Reed grinned, as if he sensed her longing to grab his offering and run with it then pinched her chin. "Try hard. Good night, Lily."

"Good night."

Waiting on the porch as Reed backed out of the drive, Lily resisted the urge to run her fingers over her tingling chin. There was no doubt she loved his touch, whether it was a soft caress, a light graze, or a sting-inducing pinch. He lifted a hand then drove down the street, leaving her to ponder how selfless his actions had been each night they'd gotten together. His focus had been on her, and only her needs to the exclusion of his own. That alone made him stand out from every man she'd ever dated, and sealed her decision to give what was brewing between them a chance. She'd wasted enough of her life rethinking and regretting her marriage.

Feeling good about her decision, she pivoted to

go inside then paused when a car went by. The driver looked suspiciously like Pam even though her head was averted and the corner street light didn't cast much illumination this far from it. Other than when John had spouted his empty promises, Lily couldn't recall a single person who annoyed her as much as Pam had in the last six weeks. If all Pam wanted was for Lily to accept her apology, she would do so first thing in the morning if it meant putting an end to this unnerving stalking.

She fell asleep with her body still tingling from Reed's touch and awoke groggy after tossing and turning all night, her skin warm with hypersensitivity. All of that boosted her eagerness to see him again later. In the meantime, the laundry and groceries wouldn't get done by themselves, but first on her list of chores was to call Pam. She picked up her cell phone from the charger next to the bed, sat down, and decided what to say as it rang.

"Hello? Lily?"

"Yes. Pam, did you drive by my house last night?"

Pam met her blunt question with a long pause before answering. "Yes. I didn't know you saw me. When I came up your street, I noticed a guy in your driveway."

Lily thought she detected a trace of accusation in Pam's voice, and her comments didn't explain anything, both of which put her on the defensive. "And? He left, so why didn't you stop? Your behavior is creepy, which is making me second-guess my decision to accept your apology and move on from what happened between you and John."

"Shit. I'm sorry, Lily. I lost my nerve to approach you again. Have I blown it, or can we mend fences?"

"I'll be honest, Pam," she replied, standing to pace barefoot across the carpeted floor. "I can forgive you easy enough since walking in on you with my husband was the catalyst I needed to end my marriage. I'm over all of it and happy, so, yes, I forgive you. If by mending fences you mean hanging out as friends again, then no, I can't go that far. Not because I'm holding a grudge but because you would be a constant reminder of the mistakes I made for way too long. So, please, don't come by again."

"But if we happen to bump into each other around town, you won't snub me?"

Pam's now hopeful tone tore at Lily's conscience, but she held firm. "No, but don't…"

"Thanks, Lily. That means a lot and all I wanted. Have a good weekend."

She hung up before Lily could warn her about

instigating any chance encounters and started to text her when her phone pealed with a call. Seeing Delia's name, she sighed, wishing she could get on with her day without dealing with anymore odd behavior from either her ex-best friend or her building friendship with Delia who used to be a casual acquaintance before John died. At this rate, she would never be able to put him and those years behind her.

"Hi, Delia. What's up?" she asked, hoping to move her along.

"Good morning. Want to get together tonight, maybe watch a movie? I can bring something to eat."

"I'm sorry, I can't. I have a date." Sort of, if she counted Reed's invite to join him at Casey's tonight as a date.

"Hey, good for you. Anyone I know?"

Everyone in the area had heard about the Kincaids despite Casey's sons keeping a much lower profile than their playboy father. It would be only a matter of time before news of the middle brother in a relationship got around. "Maybe not know, but you've heard about his family. Reed Kincaid."

"John's partner?"

Lily was surprised she knew that and at the disapproval in her tone. "Yes," she replied without further comment that would keep her on the phone. "Maybe another time. I gotta get started on chores and shopping. Bye."

"Have fun. Bye."

Shaking her head at having to deal with the odd behavior from both Pam and Delia this morning, Lily hung up and went to start coffee. She needed a large cup this morning.

Chapter Eight

Reed drew a beer for a customer while keeping watch for Lily. He'd been tempted to call her all day, find out for sure if she planned on joining him tonight at Casey's, but he wanted this decision to be hers after he'd gone to her place unannounced last night. Taking his brother's advice about Lily had been the smartest decision he'd made since hearing she had returned. He'd enjoyed sitting and watching a movie with her as much as he had bringing her to orgasm, a first for him and an evening he wanted to repeat over and over again. When he pictured himself twenty, thirty years older trying to solve a whodunit with her, he welcomed the idea. Slade would run away from a woman who threatened his solitary life, and Brett had tried, fought his attraction until he almost lost Allie to their exes' schemes.

He had already spent years longing for Lily yet doing the right thing by not acting on his attraction. Not only because she was already committed to someone else but because that someone else was his friend and partner. When their relationship had fallen apart followed by John's unexpected death, Lily had needed to come to terms with that loss. Once fate tossed them together again at the charity auction, he found it impossible to stay away.

Now, the solution seemed so simple. Reed wanted her, and she showed signs of returning his feelings, leaving nothing standing in the path of him pursuing the relationship he'd desired for so long.

"Who do you keep watching for?" Brett asked as he and Allie stepped up to the bar.

"Am I that obvious?" Somehow, that didn't bother him anymore.

"Pretty much, yeah," Allie answered for Brett as she slid onto a stool. Leaning forward on her elbows, she teased, "Have anything to do with your visit to Lily's last night? I must say, I was disappointed you were home before midnight instead of this morning."

Reed looked at Brett who shrugged. "I happened to mention where you'd gone when we returned from dinner with Allie's brother's family and saw you pulling into your garage."

"Don't worry, Reed. I got the lecture about staying out of your business," Allie said as he handed them their drinks. "But if it is Lily you're waiting for, you best invite her to your birthday party next week unless you'd rather your mother did it."

"Mom doesn't butt into our relationships," he insisted, but Allie's smirk made him think she had mentioned Lily to his mother. "What did you tell her?"

Brett set his bottle down with a thunk, glaring at his fiancée. "Allie, I warned you."

"Why is it you both think the worst of me before asking? Andrea is the one who said she wished Slade and Reed were seeing someone special they could invite. All I did was mention how much time Reed spent with Lily here at Casey's."

"The innocent look is lost on both of us," Reed told her just as Lily entered. "I planned to invite her if she showed up tonight, and there she is, so not a word out of you."

"I'll bartend now. You can spell me in a little while." Brett stood and traded places with Reed as he came around. "Had I known you invited Lily tonight, I would have insisted that Slade come out. Jordon never asks for a night off, and I think he's planning on proposing to Bianca."

"That was my understanding, and it's about time. Inviting Lily out tonight was a last minute decision and no big deal. I told her I was filling in for

Jordon, but I appreciate the short break."

Reed caught Lily's attention as he navigated his way through the crowd to meet her at the door, his gaze taking in the snug fit of her white skirt around her waist and hips. She pivoted away from the doorway, her skirt flaring around her thighs and knees, drawing his eyes below the hem to her bare legs. The distracting image of her slender limbs wrapped around his waist as he pounded into her snug heat popped into his head. He quickly squashed that mental picture, and his lust, the same as he'd done the other times they were together. His long-term goal was more important right now than appeasing his physical need.

So she wouldn't make the mistake of thinking their relationship was temporary and could sweep it under the rug, he cupped her face and kissed her long and deep first. He ended the kiss with a nip to her lower lip then soothed the bite with a stroke of his tongue, the bemusement in her whiskey eyes tickling him.

"I'm glad you came."

"I could tell," she teased him, licking her lip. "You're a very demonstrative man, Reed Kincaid, and good at keeping a girl on her toes."

"I'm only interested in keeping you on your

toes, hence, staking my claim. Brett is spotting me for a few minutes. Do you want to dance before I relieve him?"

She shook her head, sending her long braid swinging. "No, I'll play it safe and sit at the bar with you."

"Play it safe from what?" he asked, taking her hand. Her bright red halter top dipped in the front, offering a peek of cleavage as distracting as her bare legs. Of course, he had wanted her just as much clad in worn cutoffs and a T-shirt in the yard and dressed in slacks and a blouse at the fundraiser.

It was never the clothes but the woman who had drawn him since first meeting her.

She blushed and averted her face. "Never mind. Let's just visit."

With luck, Reed's plan to put off sex until next weekend, when he asked her to stay at his place after the party, would pay off in gaining her full trust. He hoped the delay demonstrated the difference between him and John, and didn't make her edgy and confused. Telling Lily he wanted more was fine, but getting her to believe him required proof. And a lot of cold showers for him.

The barstool next to Allie was still vacant, and Reed helped Lily onto it as Allie greeted her. "I'm glad you came back, Lily. How's it going?"

"Good," she answered. "Your big day is approaching fast."

"It is, finally. We'll be in next week to finalize everything."

Brett grinned at Reed. "And Slade won't be able to get out of dressing up. He's still griping about that part."

"Your brother doesn't like weddings?" Lily asked him.

"Slade's idea of socializing is attending a play party upstairs or putting his time in down here," Reed told her. "He's dreading donning a tux and being nice to a lot of people he doesn't know. What can I get you?"

"A screwdriver, please, light on the vodka. I'm driving."

A shadow crossed Lily's eyes, reminding him she and Vickie had returned to a dark house when they were last at Casey's. "Stay until I close, and I'll follow you home," he stated, now worried about her making that drive alone at night. Why hadn't he thought of that last night? It was along that stretch of highway where Allie had been rammed from behind after leaving Casey's and ended up run off the road.

Lily shook her head, her jaw set, and he realized

his mistake in ordering instead of asking. There were those who believed Lily allowed men to walk all over her because she put up with John's failings for so long, but Reed knew better. Ninety-five percent of the time she was sweet, caring, and went along with others. She'd proven in the past she possessed a rigid backbone the other 5 percent of the time.

"I can get home by myself, Reed, and plan to get up early."

Reed braced his hands on the bar top and leaned forward until his mouth was two inches away from hers. "I care about your welfare. Get used to it." He gave her a quick kiss then said, "I'll get your screwdriver."

Allie grinned at Lily. "He's almost as hot as Brett."

"I heard that, Allie," Reed tossed over his shoulder.

Brett squeezed her hand. "Don't worry, Allie. Reed's used to coming in second to me."

"You'd like to think that," he retorted, returning with Lily's drink. "Who won the javelin throw in track every year?"

"I won my freshman year," Brett returned with smirk.

"Only because I was still in middle school." He

turned to Lily who watched them with a small smile. "How is Levi? Still traveling a lot?"

"Quite a bit. When I get a weekend off, which won't happen for a while, I plan on driving up to Cheyenne for a visit."

Allie mentioned her brothers, and talk turned to sibling rivalry until Reed moved down the bar to take more orders and left her visiting with Allie. To his pleasure, she hung around after Brett and Allie went upstairs, the wistful look on her face when Allie mentioned where they were going not lost on Reed.

Feeling her out, he kept his voice low and asked, "Are you interested in coming to a play party? We're planning one soon to celebrate Jordon and Bianca's engagement, and you can attend as my guest."

She ran a finger up and down her cold glass, her cheeks turning pink. "I'm not sure. I've never given anything like that a thought."

"We can discuss it more next weekend if you come to my surprise birthday party I'm not supposed to know anything about." He couldn't tell which invitation initiated her smile of delight, but he would take either one.

Despite the thrill that shot through her when Reed mentioned taking her to a play party, Lily cautioned herself not to move so fast with entering into another relationship, remembering the mistake of doing so with John. Yet, they were friends as long as she'd been married and before Reed ever touched her intimately. While she'd spent so much time and energy focusing on her marriage until John had killed every ounce of her love, she'd never thought of Reed as anything except a friend, someone she'd grown comfortable around and liked. Now, when he gazed at her as if she was the only person in the room who mattered, she ached for him in a way she'd never desired anyone else. Any innocent touch ignited an inferno of lust she wanted only him to douse. Every protective, caring gesture or remark from Reed revealed the stark difference between demonstrating deep feelings and John's way of saying the words without backing them up.

The last of her hesitancy went up in smoke, and she answered him with all honesty. "Thank you. I'd like to come to your birthday party, and to learn more about your private gatherings." Picturing herself bound and naked in that room with other people around gave her a hot flash of either mortification or excitement, or both. She couldn't tell and figured she would have to attempt the experience to find out for sure.

Reed flashed her one of his devastating smiles that creased his tanned face and revealed his dimples, causing her heart to thump against her chest. "It's a date. Think about spending the night at my place. Be right back."

Lily's throat went dry as he strolled down the bar to take an order, the implication he was done waiting to take sex to the next level filling her pussy with damp heat. *Yes!* No other response came to mind hearing that, and she thought it best if she left now before acting a fool by begging him to take her upstairs again tonight.

"You're ready?" he asked when he returned and saw her standing, holding her purse.

"Yes. Like I said, I have a busy day tomorrow. I spend half the day at the homeless shelter and put together a dish or dessert in the morning to add to their meal."

"Okay. Let me get Eric to take over here while I walk you out."

"He's the bouncer? I'm fine, Reed. You don't need to take him away from his duties." She disliked imposing on anyone.

"Wait for me."

His tone brooked no argument, one he rarely used with her, and only when he was concerned or had her best interest at heart. Instead of getting annoyed as he spoke with Eric, she found comfort in his protectiveness. He took her hand and led her outside, another one of those gestures that elicited a warm fuzzy, his callouses spreading tingles of awareness throughout her body.

Reed opened her Mazda's door, surprising her when he asked, "What happened to the elderly Asian woman you arranged a room for during a winter snow a few years ago?"

"Hanh? How do you know about her?"

Reed brushed a hand down her spine. "I never said anything to John, but I was downtown when I spotted you helping her that day. Seeing your kindness restored my faith that there are still good people in the world."

A light bulb went off in her head, the coincidence astonishing her. "You're the one who paid for the extra nights."

He nodded. "I went in after you left and spoke with the manager. When I returned at the end of the month, I was told her family picked her up but that's all anyone knew."

"We finally located her daughter, who wasted no time to come get her mother. Hanh was separated from her family when they fled Vietnam after her husband was killed. Her children were eighteen and twenty, and she was haunted about their fate. Both daughters had married, making it harder to find them." Tears pricked her eyes as she recalled the family's reunion. "We held a celebration at the shelter."

As if he couldn't help himself, Reed crushed her against him and kissed her just long enough, slow enough to leave her yearning for more, damn him. She slid behind the wheel, frowning at him.

"You did that on purpose."

"So I did," he admitted, his voice gruff. "I won't follow you if you'll call or text me when you get home. Deal?"

"I will," she returned, glad he wasn't insisting. Lily wanted to get over fretting about her mugging without bringing up the incident. No point in riling him over something he couldn't do anything about.

"Thank you. Good night, Lily."

He shut the door and stepped back, waiting until she drove away before she watched him go inside from the rearview mirror. She drove home wondering if she would have held onto her marriage for so long if Reed had exhibited such dominant doting back then. The fact he was the opposite of John when it came to crossing boundaries with someone in a committed relationship was another trait that helped knock down her defenses.

Lily breathed a sigh of relief when she pulled into her driveway and saw the lights glowing. Between the emotional roller-coaster ride she couldn't seem to get off of and her unappeased lust, she assumed sleep would elude her, but, thankfully, she dropped off without a problem.

****

I'm not crazy.

That's what Lily told herself the next morning as she stood with her hands on her hips, eyeing the shelves bracketing the fireplace. She was darn proud of her first attempt to build anything with her own two hands, all by herself, despite the unevenness of the individual shelves. Levi had grinned without commenting, and Vickie'd laughed.

She checked the titles on her mystery movie collection again and shook her head. For sure, *Murder on the Orient Express* and *Clue* had somehow gotten switched around, and they weren't the only ones. As anal as she was when it came to keeping the eighty-plus DVDs in alphabetical order to enable easy finding when the mood for a certain title struck, she couldn't imagine making such a mistake. If Levi had been here recently, she would blame him. He loved to tease her, especially about her obsession with mystery movies and books. But everything had been in proper order when Reed was here the other night, so this had happened sometime between then and now.

Lily grew uneasy, casting a look around the room for any other anomalies but found none. That reassurance didn't stop the jitters crawling under her skin. Checking the time, she muttered, "A puzzle to be solved later." She mulled over Reed's invitation for next weekend as she put the misplaced DVDs back in their proper places. Excitement hummed inside her at the thought of staying the night with him, replacing her jumpy nerves and giving her something else to think about. No doubt about it, Reed Kincaid was a pleasant distraction from unexplainable incidents, one she could get used to if she was brave enough to let it go that far. Something else to ponder later when she wasn't pressed for time.

She padded into the bedroom and dressed in a pair of navy-blue spandex capris with a pink stripe down the sides and a bright pink collared tunic shirt. The mid-seventies forecast would make the afternoon perfect for shorts and yard work when she finished at the shelter, she thought, planning to change when she got home.

Her phone rang as she walked out of the house, double checking the lock, and she answered Ina Henderson's call, curious why the proprietor would contact her. "Hello," she said, opening the car door.

"Lily, dear, it's Ina. Would you happen to be going in to the shelter this morning?"

She wondered who'd mentioned her volunteer work to Ina. "Yes, I'm leaving now. How did you hear about my involvement, if you don't mind me asking?"

"Not at all," she returned with a chuckle. "Reed said something, oh, I don't remember when. It's been a while. If you have time to swing by and pick it up, we'd like to donate some leftover food we made last night. We usually don't have extra on weekends, just sometimes during the week, which we drop off. We're swamped this morning, or I'd run it in myself."

"No problem, Ina," she replied, realizing the restaurant was a regular donor like a few others in Casper. "Thank you. I'm on my way if you can bring it out to me in about ten minutes."

"Can do. I'll watch for you."

Ina carried out three large foil pans when Lily parked in front of the restaurant. Hopping out, she opened the back door, saying, "That's a lot of leftovers. I'm guessing you made extra. Everyone will be thrilled with whatever smells so good."

"Giving back to the community that has supported us for so long is the least we can do. No one should go hungry in this day and age." Ina placed the food on the seat then faced her with a wide smile. "Hear you're Reed's date for next weekend. 'Bout time that boy found a nice girl like you."

Lily shook her head ruefully at the quick spread of a simple invitation. "How did you hear that? He just mentioned it last night."

Ina patted her arm in a motherly fashion, blue eyes twinkling behind wire-framed glasses. "Small town gossip. Gotta love it. One of my early morning customers was at Casey's last night and somehow got wind of Reed's interest in you and invitation. His mother is one of my dearest friends, so Howard and I will see you there."

Lily would decide later if she agreed with Ina and liked the fast spread of gossip now that she lived in Eagle's Nest. "I'm looking forward to it. Thanks again."

Ina wasn't the only one who seemed happy about Reed asking her out. The next day at work, Trina threw her arms around her in a spontaneous hug that made Lily laugh. Delia called to ask about getting together and responded with an enthusiastic "you go, girl" after hearing her plans. When Saturday rolled around and Reed arrived to pick her up, she figured everyone within a fifty-mile radius had heard Reed Kincaid was seeing his former partner's widow. A tight cramp formed in her stomach when she imagined not seeing him again, which ought to decide for her how she felt about that. Instead, she kept wobbling back and forth, still undecided if she had it in her to give a serious, committed relationship another try.

Glancing out the front window, she saw him get out of his truck, her pulse leaping despite having seen him on Wednesday when he'd taken her to lunch and talking to him on the phone every day this week. His lowered Stetson shielded his potent gray-green gaze, but that chiseled jaw, firm mouth, and loose-limbed stride in snug denim were enough to dampen her palms and reawaken the need she seemed to have developed for him, and only him.

Lily rubbed her palms down her jean-clad thighs before greeting him on the porch. "Good morning. It's a beautiful day for your surprise party."

"And we'll take advantage of the nice weather. It's perfect for riding." He nodded toward the row of colorful perennials she'd finished planting along the driveway. "Nice choice of colors."

She smiled, proud of the new garden. "I had help picking them out at the nursery. Do you know what they have planned today?"

"I'm sure Brett and Slade will cook out. We'll have time for that ride I mentioned before I make my mother happy and act surprised by her efforts." He took her hand and pulled her in for a kiss, a hello she doubted she would ever tire of. She struggled to get her libido under control as he led her to his truck and opened the door. To distract her from the heat his simple kiss had generated, she settled on the seat, reminding him, "You do recall I told you it's been years since I rode a horse, right before my parents died? I was eleven."

"No problem. You'll ride with me."

Reed shut the door, and Lily watched him stroll around to the driver's side, her heart thudding with anticipation for the close press against his body as they rode. She'd been looking forward to his party until he said that; now she wished they could spend the day alone so she wouldn't have to wait until tonight to appease her lust.

"We'll go straight to the stables," Reed said, turning off the highway to enter the Kincaid Ranch between two open gates. "Slade told me to make myself scarce until noon after I told both him and Brett I was aware of Mom's plans."

Lily laughed. "Your invite last week hit the gossip circuit in Eagle's Nest the next morning. I imagine you and your brothers bear the brunt of your father's colorful lifestyle, even if you haven't followed in his footsteps."

Reed parked in front of a large stable then turned to her with a serious expression. "We haven't. I hope you believe that, Lily."

"If I didn't, I wouldn't be here." Since John first introduced them, she'd never heard a rumor about the women Reed went out with, and their private parties weren't public knowledge. None of the brothers were known for going from one woman to another as easily as changing clothes.

Lily gazed at the acres of grassland spreading as far as she could see, the faint outline of mountains along the blue skyline, and smattering of pines and aspens native to the state. "It's beautiful out here, Reed."

"Come on. Apollo and I will show you more."

"Apollo?" she asked, getting out of the truck.

He placed a hand on her lower back, his fingers brushing her skin where her short, button-up crop top left an inch of waist bare. The saddled, tethered stallion he led her toward distracted her from the warm tingles his innocent touch wrought.

"I got him as a young colt. He's eight now, and the best mount I've owned." Reed placed her hand on the horse's brown-spotted white neck, and the stallion turned to give her a friendly shoulder nudge. "And he loves the girls."

Lily chuckled, enjoying the ripple of muscle and his sleek coat against her palm as she stroked Apollo. "He's sweet, and big." It was a stretch to scratch behind his twitching ear.

"Big enough to carry both of us. I'll give you a boost up then mount behind you. Grab the pommel as you swing your leg over."

Lifting her foot onto his cupped hands, she took a deep breath and swung astride the saddle with Reed's upward push, the height disorienting her for a second before the stunning view left her speechless. She did remember to hold on tight as he settled behind her, the press of his wide chest against her back and thick arm coming around her waist distracting her from the sweeping vista of wide-open rangeland backed by the far-off mountain's hazy silhouette.

Reed pulled the reins to the left, his bulging

biceps brushing the side of her breast as he steered Apollo around the corral. He must have mistook her shudder for unease instead of physical awareness because he leaned down to whisper in her ear, "Don't worry, I've got you."

I'm beginning to believe you had me the moment I saw you dressed as Don Juan. Maybe the attraction had always been there but she'd been too blinded by love for John at first and then more concerned for her cheating husband's feelings than her own to see it. Lily sighed, relaxing against Reed, admitting it wouldn't have mattered. She wasn't ready before now, and her chest still constricted when she thought of opening herself to the ups and downs and possible pain of a relationship.

"What's going through your head, Lily?"

Swaying with the slow walk lulled her into answering without thinking. "Life's funny circles, and how mine brought me to you." She paused then added with honesty, "And questioning whether I can handle you, and what you want."

"I will never hurt you, at least not deliberately. Today, all you have to handle is a good time, starting with a run. Hold on tight. Ready?"

Once again, Reed proved he could put Lily's mind at ease with just a few words. "Ready," she replied, unsure if she meant for a faster gait or him.

Chapter Nine

Reed nudged Apollo's sides with his booted heels, the signal the stallion had been eagerly awaiting. He squeezed Lily's waist as they took off, his steed's hooves pounding into the ground, mane and tail flying, legs eating up the ground. Lily's exuberant laugh reached his ears and he bent forward, pressing them both lower so they weren't straining against the wind, her nails digging into his forearm. He couldn't detect any fear as Apollo took them over acres of grassy terrain, the trees blurring as they whizzed by them until the ranch's largest lake came into view. Spreading over one hundred and fifty acres, the blue water shimmered under the sun, reflections of the tree-covered mountain slopes undulating on the surface. Spotting a group of white-tailed deer enjoying a drink, Reed slowed Apollo from a gallop to a canter.

Once he reined to a halt, he could hear Lily's heavy breathing, feel her muscles quivering. "Is it safe to say you enjoyed that ride?"

She shifted her face up to his, their mouths a scant few inches apart, her eyes shining, her breath a warm caress as she replied, "It was freaking awesome. Will Apollo be rested enough to run like that on the way back?"

"Oh, yeah, it doesn't take him long before he's ready to go again. He enjoys splashing in the lake, so we'll hang around long enough for him to do that after the deer move on. Next time you come out, I'll load our paddle boat or a canoe in the truck, and we'll drive down here for lunch on the water."

Lily laughed when Apollo snorted and stomped his hooves. "I don't think your horse likes being left out."

"I'll give him an extra carrot." Reed clicked, and they started toward the lake as the deer took off.

Facing forward again, she stated, "You already sound sure I'll come here again. Just how far do you see this going between us?"

He didn't have to think too long or hard on his answer. "I'm in this for the long haul, so how far is really up to you."

Instead of answering, she squealed when Apollo kicked up his legs in the water with such vigor the spray reached their faces. It wasn't until they returned to the stable and he lifted her down that she brought it up again.

Leaning against him, she left her hands on his shoulders and lifted her gaze to his face. "Right now, I can't say for sure if I'm ready for another commitment, Reed, but I am open to the possibility."

"That's a hell of a lot more than you were when you left, so I'll take it." His phone beeped, and he pulled it from his pocket as she moved away. He spoke a minute with Brett then told Lily, "Time to test my acting skills. I'll get him unsaddled and turned out then we'll drive to Brett's place."

Reed figured he did a good job since his mother looked pleased with his feigned reaction when they entered Brett's house. He should have realized she would be more focused on Lily than him though. Andrea's desire for the last five years had been to see her sons settled down and working on giving her grandchildren. Once the surprise greeting dwindled and guests wandered out to the patio, she hooked her arm through Lily's with a wide smile. "Come tell me about yourself, while we carry food outside."

"I'll be happy to help. This is a beautiful home," Lily replied, sending Reed a bemused look as his mother drew her toward the kitchen.

"We'll meet outside," Reed told her. "Mother,

behave."

Andrea kept walking through the dining area off the den as she replied, "Why, whatever do you mean, Reed? Like you said, we'll catch up with you outside."

Brett's heavy hand landed on his shoulder, preventing him from following them. "Give it up, Reed. It won't do any good. Trust me, I know. Besides, Mom's harmless and means well."

"Yeah, I know, but Lily is still on the fence about committing to a relationship, and I'm ready to leap forward. I don't want Mom to push her into backing away. Lily's face is easy to read; what's going on in that head of hers is harder."

The bi-folding patio windows spanning one side of the den were open to the wide expanse of the stone-paver patio, giving Reed a clear view of his mother in an animated discussion with Lily at the buffet table. At least Lily was smiling instead of looking uncomfortable from whatever she was hearing as she placed the two pans she carried with the rest of the food.

"We had to push you toward her, and you've already decided on a future? What does that tell you?" Brett asked with a smirk.

"That you should have butted out," he returned.

"Now, as the birthday boy, I get certain privileges, one of which is keeping my girl with me."

"Good luck with that. I'll help Slade and Jordon on the grill."

They strolled outside together, Reed grateful his family had kept the gathering small today. His mother likely believed he wouldn't suspect a surprise party at thirty-nine, and, from William's nod of approval when he'd glanced toward his stepfather and mother upon entering, he'd succeeded in allowing her to keep thinking that. Because he loved his mother and Lily was still smiling with interest in whatever Andrea was relaying, he took a few minutes to chat with two cousins and a few ranch hands before going over there.

Jeff and Keith walked over ten minutes later as his cousins joined the volleyball game on the lawn. Reed pushed aside his impatience with the delay in going to Lily and greeted them. "Hey, guys. Thanks for coming."

Grinning, Jeff quipped, "Free food and lots of it. Oh, and happy birthday."

"Thanks, and I hear you. There's enough to feed a group twice this size." His stomach rumbling, he eyed the food-laden table a few feet away under the covered patio, the casserole dishes still covered.

Keith cast a quick glance toward Slade at the grill. "Good. Allie will give us take-home boxes. Is it okay with you if we take plates to Evan and Riley?"

Evan's glare when Reed and Lily returned from their ride had reminded him of the consequences for their smoking infraction. He couldn't figure out what Evan's problem was, glad the kid was Slade's headache, but as the guest of honor, he took the liberty of answering for his brother.

"Sure. Enjoy yourselves first then go ahead. I'm guessing you know what they like."

"Thank you. Like us, they aren't picky. Come on, Jeff, I'm starving."

"You don't have to tell me twice. Later, Reed."

Reed detoured to the grill to inform Slade about the food for Evan and Riley, his short reply of "That's fine," what Reed expected. His mother and Lily had taken seats on the outdoor swivel rockers, Andrea's face reflecting happy approval at his approach.

"Lily is just lovely, dear," she said, rising. "I'm going to join her at the shelter next weekend and lend a hand."

Lily stood also, looking pleased with his mother's announcement.

Taking her hand, he stated, "I'm sure they can use the extra help, but William will say you already have a full calendar with your charities and socials. Just reminding you."

She waved an airy hand, unconcerned. "I can spare a few hours now and then. Lily will let me know when they're shorthanded." She patted Lily's shoulder.

"Burgers up!" Jordon announced loudly from the grill. "Come on, birthday boy. You and Lily grab yours first."

Reed chuckled when Keith and Jeff stopped in their tracks on their way to the grill. "Come on, Lily. You, too, Mom."

****

In the eighteen years since Lily's parents had passed away, she'd never imagined another person filling their role or the void in her life their deaths caused. It should bother her that she found Reed's mother, Andrea, so appealing as a mother figure, but it didn't. Lily liked Andrea's openness, her obvious love for her sons, the way she sacrificed after splitting from their father to ensure the three boys maintained as much normalcy between the two homes as possible. Andrea had made it easy for Lily to speak candidly about her own marriage and pain in dealing with infidelity.

"That's one thing you would never have to worry about, dear," Andrea had said, patting her arm as they rocked on the porch. *"None of my boys would cheat, not after suffering through their father's sordid reputation and because I raised them to respect women."*

Of course, Reed's mother had the smarts to walk out early instead of hanging on, like Lily had done for way too long. Her ignorance in hoping John's love for her would eventually take precedence over his need for other women had become easier to admit and then put away ever since she'd laid eyes on Reed again.

He gave a short tug on her hand, tightening his grip enough for the callouses on his palm to scrape hers and send tingles up her arm, her nipples puckering in reaction. She almost tripped behind him, her gaze sliding from his broad shoulders, down his rock-hard waist to linger on his taut buttocks shifting in the snug-fitting denim. With her heart thumping double time and her sheath fluttering with a damp need that had been building for weeks, Lily decided she wasn't waiting for tonight. She was done second-guessing whether this relationship could go the long haul, or if she was even up to the challenge of another commitment. Now, today was all that mattered, and that's how she intended to go forward each day with Reed.

Her mouth watered when they reached the massive grill covered with sizzling burgers, most with melted cheese on top. Slade nodded at her as he scooped one on a bun and slid it onto Reed's plate before asking, "Cheese or no cheese, Lily?"

"Cheese please." She held out her plate, wondering if she would have room for sides dishes.

Reed winked at her from under his lowered Stetson. "That's my girl. I like your appetite."

Lily turned warm at his use of the word appetite and tried to read his expression and tone for a double meaning behind it but couldn't. Sometime soon, she would ask Allie if she knew the secret to the way the men could do that with such ease.

"I figure someday it will catch up to me, and I'll have to watch it more closely, but not today." Smiling at Slade, she said, "Thank you. They look great, and filling!"

"Save half for later tonight," Andrea said, holding her plate out for a burger. "Thank you, dear."

"Good idea," she returned, wondering if Reed's mother called everyone dear. Bianca joined them just then, her engagement ring winking in the sunlight as she laid her hand on the back of Jordon's shoulder, reminding Lily that Jordon had just proposed. "Congratulations, Bianca. May I see your ring?"

"Oh me, too," Andrea chimed in.

Jordon rolled his eyes. "Whenever Bianca sees someone she knows, we have to flash the ring." He released a dramatic sigh, but the twinkle in his eyes gave away his good humor. "Good thing I splurged on the larger diamond."

Bianca beamed, holding out her hand. "You've never held back on spending, just on taking this step." She kissed his cheek.

"You wanted to wait, also, so don't give me that."

"It doesn't matter how long it takes to be sure," Reed stated, releasing Lily's hand to rub up and down her arm in a light caress, the simple touch eliciting distracting tingles of pleasure. "When it's right, it's right."

That was my thought when I jumped to accept John's proposal.

Lily shivered from the heated glance Reed gave her, realizing the night-and-day differences between him and John. Reed consistently put her needs and wants first, whereas her husband's desires had always been his top priority. It was a heady experience being the main focus of a man's attention, one she longed to take to the next level now that she was comfortable in the relationship. She wasn't a flirt and possessed little experience in initiating sex, the only obstacles keeping her from dragging him away from the party and jumping his bones.

Lily put that thought aside, giving Bianca her attention. "Your ring is beautiful." The happiness on both Bianca's and Jordon's faces made her wish Vickie wouldn't keep Levi waiting. It saddened her that Vickie let herself become influenced by Lily's marriage struggles and failure, admitting she'd done the same since leaving John.

"Gorgeous. When?" Andrea asked without mincing words.

Slade shook his head. "Give them time, Mom."

Brett and Allie joined them, and Reed moved his hand to her lower back as talk turned to wedding dates and plans. Halfway to the food table, he caused her to stumble and go hot from head to toe when he leaned down to whisper, "Keep looking at me that way and I'll put you over my knee."

An image of lying over his lap, his hand raised above her bare pink butt, popped into her head. Lily's gaze flew up to his face to see if he was serious. Given the way her pussy dampened with a tight clutch, she half hoped so. Those sexy lips curled at the corners, but the gleam in his eyes she could barely detect with his hat lowered left her guessing.

Before Lily could form a reply, they were in line at the food table, and he changed the subject. "Save room for cake," he reminded her as she switched her attention to the array of side dishes.

Lily willed her body under control, replying, "Thanks for the reminder," then reached for the spoon in the coleslaw. She managed to gain some semblance of composure by the time they sat down across from each other at a picnic table and she eyed his loaded plate. "Will you have room for cake after eating all that?"

He removed his Stetson, the look in his eyes as arousing as his touch. "I have a healthy appetite, Lily, and, trust me, I'll be ready for cake after I show you Brett's gazebo out back."

"Gazebo?" His teasing innuendos sent her thoughts straight into the gutter, imagining a semi-private enclosure away from the party.

Reed bit into his burger, nodding and swallowing before replying, "He had it built last year. We can watch the sunset from there."

As nice as that sounded, she was more than ready for him to get naked with her tonight and hoped he didn't intend to wait much longer, guests or not. A month ago, she never would have entertained such an idea or believed her desire for one man could render her so needy. Others joined them at the table, a welcome distraction from her wayward thoughts. Reed introduced her to more relatives she wouldn't be able to keep straight, and she listened with half an ear to them talk until she'd swallowed the last bite of cheeseburger.

Reaching for her iced tea, she commented with a groan, "I need to walk off some of this food. Those burgers were huge."

"Gluttonous minds think alike." He picked up the plates and tossed them in a nearby trash can before taking her hand and tugging her to her feet.

Standing, she stuttered on a laugh. "We're going now?"

"Yes, now." Hauling her against him, he gave her a quick, hard kiss. "That's what you want, and pleasing you, seeing to your needs, is my top priority."

Reed had her at the word "needs," and Lily didn't even care who noticed their departure, following him with her heart tripping and body quaking with enthusiasm. They strolled around the side of Brett's large ranch home and followed the gravel walk out to the gazebo, her eyes drawn to the sun inching lower on the western horizon. Painting the skyline in a blaze of glory, with shades of lavender dipping into the remaining streaks of red and yellow, the calming yet vibrant scene took her breath away, no matter how many times she watched it. Much like her continuing response to Reed from the moment they met again in line at the charity auction, she mused, sliding her gaze up to him as he opened the gazebo door.

Small white lights adorned both the outside edge of the gazebo's cone-shaped roof and all around the inside where the octagon walls connected with the high ceiling. While not bright, they offered enough illumination for Lily to search Reed's five-o'clock shadowed face and read the desire in those extraordinary eyes when he tossed his Stetson onto the padded bench. Her pulse fluttered in response to his carnal look as his gaze raked down her body, her nipples peaking, pushing against her thin bra, aching for his mouth. She wasn't a flirt and had little experience with seduction, or even instigating sex. The few men she'd dated before John weren't shy about getting her into bed, and her husband had a one-track mind, never giving her the chance to come on to him.

Reed sat down on the bench and pulled her between his knees, keeping a grip on her hand. "What's going through your head, Lily?"

Talk about seductive. His deep baritone resonated in the enclosed room, faint echoes of laughter, a lone wolf's cry, and the constant click of cicadas the only other sounds filtering through the thin walls.

"I'm wondering how to get the nerve to seduce you instead of the other way around this time. I have as much experience in that as I do your kink." The look of proud approval etched on his face made uttering that flaw worth the embarrassment.

"We have plenty of time for you to practice, but not tonight. Speaking of kink though…" His eyes remained glued to her face as he slowly lowered her zipper. "I believe I mentioned a spanking."

Lily wasn't quite sure whether she was dumbfounded or electrified by hearing him mention a spanking again as he worked her jeans and panties down to her ankles. She craved his hands on her again in the worst way, and, God help her, if that happened by way of butt slaps, she discovered she didn't care. The prickles his calloused palms left behind as he followed her clothes down her legs helped her come to that quick decision, and, when he bent forward to take one very slow lick between her pussy lips, it was all she could do to keep from begging.

She shuddered, mumbling his name on a breathy moan. "Reed."

Palming her butt cheeks, he asked, "Saying red will still stop me, so, is that a yes, Lily?"

"Yes."

Reed didn't give her a chance for second thoughts, maneuvering her until she lay facedown across his rock-hard thighs, her head dangling over the end of the bench. The rapid beat of her heart thundered in her ears as the blood rushed to her face, her buttocks tensing when he rested his rough palm on one cheek. "Just once, I would like to be with you without having to rush."

"Me, too." A few uninterrupted hours to roll around completely naked with him would be nice.

"Deep breath, Lily."

She inhaled and braced for a stinging blow, but he surprised her with a light tap that warmed her buttock, but that was all. Oddly let down, she didn't think before turning her head around and saying, "Is that all there is to it?"

He shook his head, muttering, "You continue to amaze me. No, there can be much more."

He demonstrated with a harder swat, one that burned, stung, and drew a gasp. The next one covered her other cheek, leaving her whole backside pulsing and her rethinking this decision until he caressed the twin sore spots, the softer touch over the sting going straight to her nipples and pussy. "Oh my."

"I'll take that as my cue to give you a few more."

Lily caught the amusement in his tone then ceased thinking with any clarity as he delivered a volley of smacks, alternating between hard and light, building a deep heat that seeped through her skin into muscle and produced a dull throbbing across both buttocks. A hiccup escaped her constricted throat, and her head swam with the myriad of different sensations and the revelation of an erogenous zone she'd never considered before. Responding with frissons of hot flutters traveling from her nipples to her sheath, shocking her with the feverish pitch of arousal, she lay helpless to do anything except go with the flow when Reed slipped a finger inside her and went straight for her clit.

Lily's tight, slick pussy muscles clamped around Reed's finger with the first touch of her clit. Her soft cry, arched back, and gyrating hips against his thighs tested his control, his cock a pulsing rock-hard pressure against his zipper. He didn't want her embarrassed if someone came looking for them, so he hurried her along, circling and teasing the swollen bud until she groaned with the final orgasmic release. Pulling from her contracting clutches was as difficult as postponing his own release for a while longer but necessary with the party still going on. He hadn't planned this scene, intending to wait until they were alone at his place, but she'd proved too difficult to resist when she kept turning those whiskey eyes full of longing on him.

"Lily, I hate to rush, but…"

"No." She shook her head, sitting up before he could help her, her hands going to his belt. "Not this time. Your guests can wait or watch. I don't care."

Desperation colored her voice, her breathing heavy as she unbuckled his belt and worked his zipper over his erection. "Are you sure?" he asked, covering her fumbling fingers with one hand and turning her face toward him with the other. "I have a condom, but we've been out here awhile."

"I'm sure," she stated, her eyes revealing a shyness despite the bravado behind her words.

He slid his hand down her leg to pull off one shoe, saying, "Then I hope you're good with fast for our first time." Working her leg out of her jeans next, he struggled to keep from shoving her hands aside and freeing his cock himself to hurry this along. Regardless of what she said, he doubted she was ready for a public scene.

"I am." His cock sprang into her hands, her eyes widening as she stroked his hot flesh. "Maybe. You may not fit." She cast him a cheeky grin then held her hand out for the condom.

"Next time. I'll embarrass myself and disappoint you if you put it on right now." Reed sheathed himself then grasped her hips as she straddled his lap. He slid with ease into her hot pussy, watching her suck in a deep breath and hold it while he worked his way through slick, tight muscles toward filling her completely. A smile blossomed across her face the second he was embedded deep inside her snug heat.

With her hands on his shoulders, she pushed down and rose until only his cockhead remained hugged by her soft folds. "You did say we had to be fast, right?" she commented, sliding back down.

Reed gritted his teeth against the searing clutch enveloping his cock through the protection, latching onto her hips to aid her movements. "Right, and you're doing a damn good job, Lily." Surprised pleasure turned her face pink, as if no one had ever complimented her during sex before. Idiots. "But it'll be better, and quicker if we work together."

"Plus, you're a control freak." She gasped as he raised her then rammed upward and lowered her in one controlled movement.

"Yes, I am. Fuck, you feel good." Her face suffused with the same delight, and he cursed his former friend who hadn't had the good sense to treat her as she deserved. "Hold tight," he instructed, setting up a steady rhythm of lift and lower, fucking her faster and faster when her wet clutches squeezed his cock with convulsive grips.

Her nails dug into his shoulders, his fingers pressing deep into the malleable flesh of her buttocks to aid in the pounding of their bodies coming together. Reed grunted with his efforts, jerking her down one more time before bursting into fiery, orgasmic pleasure, his head swimming with the rolling waves consuming his body and Lily's soft cries as she sucked him dry. It took hearing Slade's bird whistle to clear his head and ease his hold on her clenching ass. Conscious of the passing time, he forced his breathing under control, pausing only long enough for her to do the same.

"I hate to rush you," he whispered against her arched neck, the tip of her braid swinging against his fingers. "But Slade is headed this way, probably to warn us we've been missed."

Her breath released on a *whoosh*, and she lifted off his lap, giving him a red-faced grin. "That's okay. It was worth Slade getting a peek and cutting recovery time short."

Damn, but he was crazy about her.

"He just now came around the corner," Reed stated, standing and watching her pull up her clothes as he disposed of the condom in a corner trash bin. "And, for future reference, it doesn't take me long to recover, but, if possible, I won't rush you."

Lily took his outstretched hand, looking more relaxed than he'd seen her in a long while. "I have a feeling I won't need much with you, either."

"Time to cut the cake!"

"Coming!" Reed answered Slade, leaving the gazebo thinking about how much he liked Lily's unique combination of verbal openness and shy demeanor.

Chapter Ten

An alarm went off, and Lily opened her eyes to witness the bright orange and yellow blends of the sun rising above the mountains from Reed's bedroom window. His arm lay like a heavy, comforting weight across her waist, the deep rumble of his low groan vibrating against her back. She sighed, shifting her hips against his groin, the press of his hard cock between her buttocks bringing her fully awake. Her body said, yes, one more time, but the clock told her indulging in another bout of mind-numbing sex would make her late to work.

"I can't, Reed. I..."

"Have to go. I know." He rolled away and she missed the snug embrace she'd enjoyed all night. "Use my bathroom, and I'll use the one down the hall. I'll fix coffee to go and meet you in the kitchen."

"Thanks."

Lily watched him stroll out of his master bedroom buck naked, his buttocks just as taut as they'd felt last night, wishing she didn't have to leave yet. Reed was slowly becoming an addiction she didn't want to get over. After everything she'd been through with his partner, that should scare her off further involvement. Instead, she found herself looking forward to spending more time with him on his ranch, and in his bed, which she needed to get out of without delay.

Rising, she winced, her muscles unused to such rigorous sexual activity. She smiled, enjoying that telltale reminder of his intensity last night until she noticed her loosened hair. "Oh, damn," she muttered, looking for the band to tie it back again. When she couldn't find it, she swore again and grabbed her clothes. Now she would need extra time at home to get the tangles out and re-braid the long thick strands. Sometimes she wondered why she carried on this petty dig at John now that he was gone and no longer nagging her about cutting it. Maybe she should consider making another change, other than indulging in sex again.

She padded into the massive attached bath, the sea-green vanity and marbled shower in a matching shade a direct contrast with the dark wood of his bedroom. The color and sunlight streaming through the window above the large soaking tub soothed her aggravation over her hair. As much as she wanted to, she didn't have time to linger, washing up and dressing in a few minutes before finding Reed ready to drive her home, holding two coffee cups with lids.

"Thank you." She sipped the piping-hot brew, creamed and sweetened perfectly, then said, "You may have redeemed yourself from taking my hair down."

"I've never seen it loose." Reed ran a hand down her hair then continued until he pressed against her butt and gestured with his coffee-holding hand out the door. "You should wear it down more often. It's beautiful."

"It's a pain to keep from getting tangled, which you would know if you'd asked me."

"I don't ask when you are in my bed and we're having sex, as you know. You could have said red," he returned without an ounce of remorse.

Lily laughed, skipping down the front steps, and turned her head to reply. "You were distracting me with sex. How could I say anything when I didn't even realize what you did until this morning."

He shrugged, a grin curling his lips as he opened the truck door for her. "Not my fault you're distracted easily."

"There's no talking sense to you this morning."

She hopped onto the seat, unable to think of another guy she'd bantered about sex with, or anyone whose company she enjoyed so much the morning after. Not even John, whom she'd loved deeply in the beginning. She remained upbeat until they reached her house, one look at her crushed new flowers along the drive deflating her good mood. Her throat tightened with disappointment, her stomach roiling with anger at the deliberate destruction when he pulled into the drive.

"What the hell? Lily…"

Reed swiveled toward Lily but her hand was already on the door handle, and she didn't pay attention when he said her name. Jumping out, she stomped over to the flattened spring blossoms, the soil dug up from obvious tire tracks. She used one foot to push dirt off the cement into the garden bed, muttering, "This bad luck *has* to stop."

Clasping her arm, he hauled her against him, his rock-solid strength defusing her anger, forcing her to blink back tears as he asked, "What are you talking about? What bad luck?"

Lily shook her head and stepped away, wishing she could lean on him longer. "Just one mishap after another since coming home. She gestured toward the destroyed plants. "The neighbor kid probably did this. He's a reckless teenage driver."

"File a complaint. Give them his license plate number. A visit from highway patrol or the local cops usually works." Taking her hand, he led the way to the door.

"It's always been at night, up the street. I can't identify the car, or even the driver, only where he lives, on the corner." Lily unlocked the door, and Reed followed her inside. With a sigh, she tossed her purse on the small table and shoved her hair aside. "It's odd, though, because when I've seen him during the day, he's always been so nice and polite. But I don't have time to do anything about it now."

"Are you sure that's all it is, Lily, bad luck?" Reed drew her forward and she saw the suspicion on his face. "What else has happened other than your electric problem?"

He would think she was nuts if she mentioned the DVD's were out of place, and she didn't dare bring up the mugging right now. Instead, she voiced her first thought. "What else could it be? You worry too much." She smiled to ease the concern in his gaze.

"And you don't enough. I want you to tell me if you have any other issues, big or small. I mean it, Lily." He kissed her, long and deep, until she relaxed and let herself enjoy the taste of him again before he left.

An hour later, her morning got even worse when she ran into Pam coming out of Creative Events as she pulled in to park. Lily had never said anything to Trina about her issue with Pam, and was hoping she wouldn't stop by the office again before her parents' anniversary dinner and dance. Unable to avoid her, she came around the SUV, intending to be polite, but Pam put an end to that with a snarky greeting.

"I'm leaving, so don't worry. You don't have to suffer my presence."

Without another word, or even a glance, she got into her car and sped off, leaving Lily standing there feeling bad their relationship had come to this. Maybe she should have tried harder to at least get on friendlier speaking terms with her once best friend. From Pam's glacial expression, she doubted that was possible now.

Lily blew out a breath and went inside, pasting on a smile for Trina who saw right through it. Looking up from behind her desk, she asked, "What's wrong? Didn't your weekend go well?"

I've got to work on a better poker face. Striding to her desk, Lily replied, "It went great except for returning this morning to see my new flowers smashed." Trina knew she planned to spend yesterday and last night with Reed. "Someone ran over them, probably the teenager down the street."

Sunlight from the wide front window splashed across the blue carpet, reaching the blue-and-white striped chairs in front of their desks. The cheery brightness of the space lightened Lily's mood, even though she still bemoaned the destruction of her hard work and poor timing of running into Pam.

"That sucks. I'm sorry. You've endured more than your share of bad luck lately. I would ask who you pissed off, but you never do or say anything that isn't nice."

"Well, I'm about to rant against fate or coincidence or plain bad luck if this keeps up." Settling at her desk, she flipped the calendar and saw the busy schedule. "Wow, this will take my mind off everything else. How about you take the clients, and I'll start on the venue calls?"

"Between graduations and weddings, we're swamped, just how I like it. Yes, let's do that, otherwise, we'll overlap. We did just get one cancellation from Pam Davidson, her parents' fiftieth anniversary dinner dance, which makes next weekend our last weekend free of a booking until late July. Half of August is already penciled in, also, so we'll start closing on Monday instead of Saturday next week. Sound good?"

Lily nodded, remembering that schedule last year before she'd left for Florida. "Sure. It's those events that pay the bills. I'm sorry about the Davidson cancellation. That's my fault." She went on to explain the rift in her and Pam's relationship before adding, "See, I'm not such a nice person. I can't seem to forget her betrayal despite having set aside my animosity. Whenever I hear her voice or see her, it all comes rushing back."

"Now that you're in a new and much better relationship, you'll find a way to get back on speaking terms with her. Don't worry about the cancellation, we have more than enough business to tide us over during the slower winter months that get boring when I'm here alone." Trina sent her a pointed look. "No taking off again if it doesn't work out between you and Reed. Not that I think that will happen. You two have been well-acquainted for years."

"That's not the same as involved, which hasn't been for long." A pang gripped her abdomen at that suggestion. How had he become so important to her in such a short time?

Their first appointment arrived, relieving Lily.

She didn't want to discuss or think about plaguing mishaps or how her relationship with Reed might or might not pan out, not right after seeing Pam again. It wasn't until midafternoon, when things slowed down and Trina left early to attend the girls' soccer game that she returned to questioning her escalating relationship with Reed. She tried not to, tried to let it go and enjoy the ride, for however long it lasted, but couldn't. Driving home, she went over the pros and cons of dating a wealthy, sought-after man like Reed, wondering what he saw in her.

Lily preferred staying home instead of going out, spent her free time volunteering at the homeless shelter, and her only experience with kinky sex was what Reed taught her. How did he not find her boring? When she reached the turnoff for Eagle's Nest, she slowed down, in no hurry to get home and see her ruined garden, wishing she could keep driving to Reed's ranch despite the return of her misgivings. With only two appointments on the schedule for Friday, she would get off early enough to buy some more flowers and plant them in the afternoon.

Turning onto her street, her pulse flipped at seeing Reed's truck parked at the curb, tears blurring her vision when she noticed the newly planted flowers replacing the smashed ones. *This is why he so easily slipped past my insecurities.* She blinked away her emotional response to his surprise, pulled into the driveway, and didn't let his sweaty, dirt-streaked arms deter her from throwing hers around him when he opened the door.

"Thank you! It looks beautiful." His tight embrace felt as nice as coming home to his surprise. Lily leaned back and gazed at his sun-kissed face, his eyes appearing greener without his hat shielding the sunlight. "This is a great surprise. If you can stay for dinner, I have the fixings for chicken Parmesan."

"Sounds better than taking you out like I planned, and you're welcome. I picked up a white border fence you can string small lights on to prevent another accident. It won't take me long to put it in then I'll wash up and change shirts."

"No hurry. It'll take about an hour," she replied, looking forward to the evening until she saw Delia approaching. "Excuse me. That's a friend of mine." Delia appeared to be frowning when Lily walked to the curb and waved then figured she was mistaken when she pulled over, grinning.

Leaning her head out the window, Delia hurried to say, "I finished shopping at the mercantile earlier than I expected and decided at the last minute to run by and ask if you want to grab a burger, but never mind." She nodded toward Reed. "You have plans."

"Sorry about that," Lily said, not regretting Reed's visit in the least. "I can meet you somewhere for lunch this week." She shouldn't suffer a twinge of guilt at letting Delia down, nevertheless, a pang gripped her abdomen.

"We have two people gone on vacation and are short-staffed. Maybe next week. Give me a call."

Delia drove away without another word, one glance at Reed making it easy for Lily to forget about her.

Reed watched the short exchange between Lily and her friend, pondering whether there was another reason for the way Lily had seemed unhappy about her arrival other than the interruption. He couldn't shake the suspicion something was bothering her, dissatisfied with how she withheld her complete trust. Maybe his own insecurities were causing him to imagine evasive answers and eye shifts, notably when she mentioned a piece of recent bad luck. The constant urge to push for the commitment he was ready for kept him on edge, making it harder to keep himself in check. One of these days, if he failed to get more of a response from her other than a polite brush-off about these personal issues, he would explode.

Shifting his thoughts, he eyed her slender legs showcased in heels and a knee-length dress, wishing he had time to stay after dinner. Slade already wasn't happy with the way he'd taken off earlier to pick up the flowers and replace her ruined garden. Once Reed told him what happened and what he planned, Slade's attitude changed. All the same, his obligations at home were as important as his desire to ease Lily's unhappiness, and he wouldn't shirk them.

"I'll get started on dinner," Lily stated, her face reflecting nothing but pleasure. "Do you like green beans? I picked up a fresh batch at the farmer's market."

"My mother raised me to try everything on my plate. I didn't like that rule then. Now I eat and enjoy everything, including green beans."

"Levi was a stickler when it came to my diet also. However, I still won't touch a mushroom. Come in when you're done."

Reed often forgot her brother had taken over raising her when their parents died. He met Levi at John and Lily's wedding, portraying an overprotectiveness that pleased him. He made a mental note to thank him sometime if her only sibling didn't punch him for sleeping with his sister. Despite the trauma of losing her mom and dad at such a tender age, she'd grown up a sweet and compassionate woman, in part, thanks to Levi's sacrifices.

He retrieved the fencing from his truck, his stomach's rumbling prodding him to move faster. Twenty minutes later, he grabbed a clean shirt from the truck cab and caught a whiff of Lily's cooking the moment he opened the front door. He also noticed the flimsy door handle, pausing to check the lock. Shaking his head at the worthless push-button lock on the knob, he shut the door and called out, "You need a dead bolt on this door, Lily. I can pick one up for you."

"Don't you dare, Reed," she returned. "I can get one this week. You've done enough. Go wash."

He swiveled, finding her standing with hands on her hips, her face set in stone. She didn't exert her independent streak often but, when she dug her toes in, they were buried to stay rooted.

"Okay, but soon. Your safety isn't up for discussion."

There it was, that telltale wince only he would possibly notice. From this distance, he could be wrong, so he let it slide once more. He hastened into the bathroom, her muttering following him down the hall.

"There's a good chance your chicken Parmesan will piss off Slade. Just warning you." Reed leaned back in the chair with a sigh, setting his fork down on the now empty plate.

She sipped her tea, frowning before lowering the cup, cocking her head. "Why would my cooking matter to your brother?"

"Because I have chores waiting on me and might not get to them now. Damn, that was good, Lily."

Her eyes shone liquid gold from the simple praise. "Thank you. I don't get to cook for anyone except Levi and Vickie when they visit, which isn't often enough."

He thought of something he hadn't contemplated before. "Do you miss living in Cheyenne, closer to them?"

"No, not at all." She stood to gather their plates. "He still reverts to protective big brother mode too often, and we would argue a lot more. More tea?"

"I'm good, thanks."

She returned to the table carrying a plastic-covered container. "I'll send the rest home with you.

There's enough to share with Slade. Maybe he won't get mad at me, then."

"He'll love it. Thanks." Reed stood and took the container, clasping her hand with his free one. "I'm sorry I have to eat and run," he said, heading to the door where he kept the kiss short. Otherwise, he wouldn't leave. "Come out to the ranch Friday, and stay the weekend if you can."

With their faces so close, there was no mistaking the indecision and brief unease darkening her expressive eyes when she replied, "Would you mind staying here Friday night?"

Wanting answers, he cupped her chin and held her head up, facing him. "What's bothering you, Lily? And don't tell me nothing." Her jaw went rigid under his hand, her eyes narrowing in displeasure, but he wouldn't give up yet. Knowing better than to threaten, he tried to entice her into answering. "I might be able to help. I *want* to help if I can."

Her eyes widened and softened, then Lily slipped out of his light hold but didn't look away when she answered, "You did help, Reed. Coming home to the new garden took a load off my mind and shoulders. Work is busy, and I'm finding out owning an older home comes with issues I hadn't planned on. I've been going nonstop since returning.

I understand if staying in at my place doesn't appeal to you." She reached for the door and opened it. "Thanks again for what you did. It means a lot."

There was more; Reed was sure of it. But instead of pushing and risking losing the ground he'd made in developing a relationship with her, he saved it for another day. Reaching out, he gripped her braid, tugged her head back, and swooped down to cover her open mouth. She melted against him, her moan music to his ears, her easy compliance rousing his sexual dominant need to take her to the floor and fuck her until she gave him everything. It took every ounce of control to let her go, little effort to agree to her request.

"I'll let my brothers know I'm spending the weekend with you and to bring dinner Friday. Make a list of repairs or things you want checked."

Reed walked out to his truck without glancing around, the pleasure suffusing her face enough for now.

****

Reed's molten gaze traveled down her naked body, a small grin curling his lips. "You look good, bound and waiting for me."

Lily strained against his belt binding her wrists together and looped around one of her headboard's brass rods, stretching her arms, thrilling to the freedom of accepting his demands without worry or thought. She eyed the stunning eagle tattoo adorning his shoulder and upper arm then took in his thick, bare chest before gazing at his face again. The week had flown by in a flurry of work, Reed calling several times and breaking away from his obligations long enough to meet her at Ina's for dinner with Brett and Allie. His urgency had rubbed off on her the moment he arrived this evening, tugging her straight into the bedroom, turning her breathless with hot expectation as he tossed her on the bed.

"And here I thought we would do a movie first after dinner." Not that she minded sex first, loving the restriction that made it easy to go with whatever he wanted without having to think about anything else.

"The movie can wait. I can't." Bracing a hand on the headboard, he grasped her nipple between thumb and forefinger and applied pressure until the nub went numb, her eyes watering when he didn't let up. Shaking his head, he let go and circled his palm over the tortured tip. "You should have stopped me before you were so uncomfortable."

Without warning, he grasped her hip and tilted her sideways enough to deliver a sharp smack on her buttock. Lily gasped, her cheek throbbing from that one spank. Now her nipple and butt hurt, but it was the disappointment in his tone that pained her most.

"I'm sorry." She couldn't think of what else to say.

"Testing your limits is fine," he stated, toying with her other nipple, "and something I'll help you with. Just don't try too much too fast. I love your breasts, and your responsive nipples."

Lily would have thanked him except he knelt on the bed still wearing his jeans and parted her legs with his knees. The cool air wafted over her denuded heated flesh, his visual exploration between her parted labia causing goose bumps. Hot mortification took over as he slid his hands up the inside of her thighs and used his thumbs to spread her plump folds wider. It didn't help when she responded damply to the burn now pulsing on her buttock.

She shifted her legs and hips under his lasered gaze, drawing his attention up to her face. Removing his hands, he slid under her butt, lifted her pelvis, and lowered his head, saying, "You're a tempting dessert I can't resist."

"*Oh!*" His warm breath on her sensitive skin

dispelled the goose bumps yet still drew a shiver. *"Reed,"* Lily moaned as he licked up her seam, the tip of his tongue grazing her extended clit. She shook from the impact of that light touch, seeing his dark head between her lighter thighs another decadent turn-on. Oral sex was an intimacy she'd only shared with John, and, God help her, she'd never reacted so fast or desperate for more than now as Reed added a finger.

Stroking the tissues along her pussy walls, he tongued her clit again, circling first then tugging with his teeth. She jumped at the slight prick that caused her to gush and convulse around his finger, ratcheting up her arousal. He kept up the dual assault until reality faded and raw sexual hunger invaded her body, the tremors racking her body taking command of her senses. Her breath lodged in her throat, trapped but for ragged gasps. His tight grip on her cheeks forced her to endure the onslaught of pleasure spreading through her body in a heated rush since she wasn't about to end it with the safeword, not when it rivaled anything she'd felt before.

Lily still quaked with aftershocks, her sheath still throbbing with softer contractions when Reed released his hold and lifted his head. She couldn't speak, too befuddled from such a strong response to do much except watch as he rose and shucked his jeans. With a wicked grin, he placed a knee near her head, reaching up to remove the belt from her wrists. The move rubbed his cockhead against her face, close enough to her mouth all she had to do was turn her head to lap over his seeping slit, taste his tangy pre-cum on her tongue, and relish his indrawn breath.

"Better not let you do that again," he said, his voice a guttural rumble above her.

Lowering her arms, she latched onto his waist, still working at catching her breath. "Why? Don't you like oral?"

Reed huffed a laugh, lowering on top of her. "Honey, *every* man likes oral." He plucked a condom off the nightstand and ripped it open with his teeth then said, "Next time, maybe, if I'm not eager to get inside you, which might take a few hundred nights of this before I'm there. Wrap your legs around me."

What did it say about her that she got off on that deep commanding tone, loved the way his control stripped her of all inhibitions and insecurities?

"Okay...*oh God.*"

Reed surged inside her before she hooked her ankles right above his clenching buttocks, her hands coming up at the same time to grab onto his smooth shoulders. Braced on his forearms by her shoulders, he lowered his head, his warm breath tickling her neck as his hands tunneled under her head to cradle her skull. Holding her as snug as she gripped him with her arms and legs, he rained kisses across her face, lips, and over to her ear where he ended with a sharp nip on her lobe that ricocheted straight down to her pussy. Her body slickened, inside and out, and she arched against the pounding thrust of his hips, basking in every deep, plunging stroke that scraped along sensitive nerve endings and rasped her swollen clit.

"That's it, Lily. Now. Come all over me."

Unable and unwilling to deny him, Lily let go, her world splintering apart for a second time, the insane pleasure stripping her of all cognizant thought except one word – *more.*

****

Lily's antagonist stayed parked at the end of the street, seeing the newly planted garden and truck at the curb, fuming at the injustice. *She has no right to happiness, not after robbing me of mine.* Knowing what they were doing, Lily happy and sated instead of worried or scared ruined all the fun of tormenting her. Night cloaked the street in darkness except for the lone streetlight at the other end of the block. An hour passed then two, and the rage built until it became all-consuming, pushing the tormentor into taking action. With a tight grip on the knife, the enemy Lily didn't know she had quietly got out of the car and snuck up the street, careful to keep out of sight of any windows with lights shining. The misdeed only took a few satisfying minutes, long enough to inflict major damage and throttle back hot fury.

Now to plan Lily's demise.

Chapter Eleven

Reed awoke early, picked up his jeans and shirt, and left Lily sleeping in her bedroom. After dressing, he started a pot of coffee then left a note on the kitchen counter, telling her he would be right back. One of the perks small towns offered were small businesses no longer found in bigger cities, like the bakery a few blocks away. Lily was partial to their muffins and bagels with coffee.

The sun had just chased away the gray of dawn when he stepped out onto the porch, his relaxed, mellow mood evaporating the moment he saw the destructive vandalism to Lily's SUV. Shock yielded quickly to fury, every muscle tensing as he stormed toward the vehicle to check the extent of the damage. *A reckless teenager did not do this.* Squatting in front of a rear tire, he examined the deep slashes that only a sharp, good-sized blade could make. All four tires were ruined by gashes several inches long, the Mazda's frame marred with deep scrapes running along both sides, the lights jimmied loose, and the wiring cut.

His rage morphed into a slow burn and put on simmer to contain his volatile emotions. Grabbing his phone, he texted Brett and Slade, giving them a brief description, needing their help. The urge to strike out at someone before Lily awoke toned down with their fast replies. He sent another text on his way back inside, asking them to stop at the bakery first. Lily would need all the comfort he could give her.

She was pouring coffee when he entered, her hair swinging as she turned her head and smiled. "There you are. Where'd you go?" Carrying two steaming cups, she met him halfway and handed him one.

"Thanks." He sipped, bracing himself for her reaction before answering. "I planned to run to the bakery but got sidetracked and asked Brett and Slade to swing by on their way here."

"Your brothers are coming? Why?" She looked down at her loose gym shorts and T-shirt. "I should change."

Reed snatched her hand before she could head to the bedroom and tugged her over to the sofa. "Wait, Lily. Sit down, and I'll tell you."

She surprised him when she yanked her hand free, her face getting that rare stubborn look. "Quit babying me and tell me what's happened."

"Fine." He'd tried it his way, to talk to her in a slow, calm manner. Since she insisted, he would give it to her with quick bluntness. "Your Mazda was vandalized last night, all four tires are ruined, and you're looking at a hefty repair expense with the other damage. *Now* do you want to tell me... Lily, wait!" He swore as she dashed to the door, heedless of the hot coffee sloshing onto the floor.

Reed set his cup down and followed, her pale, stunned face imprinted in his mind. She was quiet, maybe too quiet, walking around the SUV, running her fingers over the damage, her eyes remaining downward at the tires. He halted where the walkway from the porch connected to the drive, giving her space and a few moments to digest the loss and deliberate sabotage. Her body was stiff, her gaze smoldering when she looked up.

"The kid down the street didn't do this."

"No, he didn't." Reed went to her, relieved she'd realized that right away. He detected the worry and hint of fear in her eyes when he stood before her, the same look he'd seen before. This time, though, he could almost feel her body vibrating with the effort to hold back the anger he'd first detected. "You need to tell me if anything else has happened."

"It doesn't make sense, Reed." Lily looked at her coffee cup as if she forgot she still held it then took a drink.

"What doesn't?" he asked, impatient for answers that might have to wait since Brett and Slade arrived, snagging her attention.

They were each carrying a box from the bakery. Brett whistled and Slade's expression grew dark when they took in the damage to her car. "It's worse than I imagined," Brett said, his gaze shifting from the Mazda to Lily. "You okay, Lily?"

She shook her head, sighing. "No, because I haven't a clue who would do such a thing, or why."

"Someone was pissed." Slade scanned the cars parked in her neighbor's driveways. "You're in the middle of the block, with houses across from you and next to you, so I doubt someone drove down this street in the dead of night and randomly picked a vehicle to take out their anger on."

Reed agreed. "Which means it's time to pick your brain. We can do that over breakfast."

"Fine, but there's not much to tell. I lead a boring life. I'll..." She paused, her eyes widening when a white Lexus whipped into the driveway behind her SUV. "Levi?"

Her brother got out and slammed the door. "You were mugged and didn't tell me? What the hell, Lily?"

Oh shit. The full weight of all four men's censoring gazes kept her immobile and silent for a few stunned seconds. At that moment, Lily discovered what a deer must experience when caught in the headlights of an oncoming car. She stood frozen, cringing inside until she noticed Vickie getting out of the passenger side of Levi's car. She'd been so surprised to see her brother show up, she hadn't glimpsed Vickie with him.

Taking advantage of the guilt on her friend's face, Lily said, "We'll discuss this inside, away from neighbors." She pointed at Vickie. "You come help me fix eggs. We'll need them to go with whatever the guys brought from the bakery."

"Lily, we're going to talk," Levi snapped.

Reed clasped her wrist as she made to pass him into the house. "Yes, Lily, we're going to talk."

What a mistake she'd made in keeping that first incident between her and Vickie. She didn't believe it had anything to do with the vandalism here at her home but admitted she should have talked to Levi about it and mentioned it to Reed after he'd seen the bruise on her shoulder. She'd spent months listening to John's evasive replies to her inquiries over suspicious behavior and knew the distrust and ache keeping secrets could produce.

"Let me fix breakfast first." She glanced around at the other three men just as Levi looked at her vehicle, his face reflecting shock. "Give me fifteen minutes," she stated quickly. "Come on, Vickie."

"Someone better tell me what the hell is going on."

Levi's furious voice followed her inside, and she shut the door right behind Vickie before turning on her friend. "Thanks a lot."

She spun toward the kitchen, Vickie right behind her in defense mode. "Hey, I tried for what, a few weeks now? He was gone so long, it took one look to get me naked and on my back then he asked about you. It slipped, sue me. You know how much he loves you."

Lily whipped around from retrieving the eggs out of the refrigerator, the envy in Vickie's tone catching her off guard. "I know, but surely you don't think his feelings for me are stronger than for you. He's crazy about you, asked you to marry him."

Vickie reached for a bowl and set it on the

counter for her. "No, that came out wrong. He has me in knots. I've never seen him so mad."

"My fault. I shouldn't have put you in that position." Lily broke a dozen eggs into the bowl, added milk, and whisked them together. "On a scale of one to ten, just how mad is he?"

"Ten, without a doubt. Do you have paper plates? I don't want to do dishes."

She pointed to a lower cabinet, turned on the stove then filled the coffee for a full pot. "There're plastic forks, too. Extra coffee cups are above you. With luck, breakfast will calm all of them down."

"I wouldn't count on it," Vickie replied, setting the plates on the counter before stepping to the coffeemaker next to the stove. "Levi is mad at you, but more upset and worried. And now your Mazda? *I'm* thinking of hiding somewhere until he calms down."

"His bark is worse than his bite. You know that."

Lily stirred the eggs in the large pan, trying not to dwell on her brother or the damage to her SUV, the expense, and why someone appeared to hate her. Waking to face that deliberate destruction of her property ruined the memory of spending another night with Reed. Even though he had donned his jeans when they got out of bed to watch a movie, he'd insisted she remain naked. Once she sat curled up on the couch with her breasts snuggled against his bare chest, his hand roaming her body while Jimmy Stewart entertained them in *Rear Window*, she found nakedness a delightful way to view one of her mysteries. Another pleasant memory tarnished by some crazed individual. Unlike Levi, she rarely lost her temper, but something like this could do it if she ever came face-to-face with the culprit.

The guys came inside as she scooped the eggs into a bowl, her combined living space and kitchen shrinking with their tall, broad-shouldered presence. Brett, Slade, and Levi tossed their Stetsons on top of Reed's on the armchair before crowding into the kitchen, still looking none too happy.

"You guys sit at the table. Vickie and I will eat at the counter."

"You will sit by me," Reed stated.

"And me." Levi glare at Reed.

Slade unleashed a rare grin. "This ought to be interesting. Brett and I are taking the counter." He didn't wait for argument, snatching a plate and scooping eggs onto it then reaching into a box to pull out a bear claw.

Brett did the same while the four of them sat

down. Lily's mouth watered when Reed handed her a blueberry scone. "Thank you. Try to get along and be nice." That second part she leveled at her brother.

Levi's scowl didn't change. "We'll discuss you taking up with a Kincaid later. Talk. You were assaulted when leaving a charity function?"

Conscious of everyone's attention zeroed in on her, she told them in a few sentences what happened. "His bat barely grazed my shoulder before the security guard came out and he took off. That's all there was to it, and I was fine." She took a bite of egg, avoiding eye contact with Reed, remembering he'd asked about the bruise when they were upstairs at Casey's.

"That's weird," Brett said.

Reed lowered his coffee to reply. "Exactly what I was thinking."

"Why is it weird? Casper has its fair share of crime, including muggings downtown. You forget, I work at the shelter, and I've seen and talked to plenty of victims of random violence."

"Because someone dressed in a Halloween costume carrying a bat would draw attention," Reed stated. "Muggers usually attack at whim, a quick assault to grab someone's belongings before taking off, and are rarely armed."

"We're thinking along the same lines, then. Odds are, the guy was lying in wait for you, which means it was not random. What happened next? Anything strange or out of the ordinary?" Brett asked.

Lily would have pegged him for a lawyer right away if he'd used that firm tone and direct line when they'd met. She was working up the nerve to mention the misplaced movies, not wanting to come across as a complete lunatic, when Vickie spoke.

"The electricity, Lily. Remember?" Vickie turned to face the guys. "We returned here after going out to Casey's one night, and every light we left on was off. It was pitch black inside, and we used our phones to get to the breaker box where we found loose wiring."

Lily shrugged, still not convinced. "I called an electrician, and he replaced all the wiring, said it was frayed and would short out again. It's an old house. There's nothing odd about that."

"What's his name? I'll talk to him."

Lily rolled her eyes, stood, and retrieved the electrician's card from a drawer, and handed it to Brett.

"Did he take the old wiring with him?" Slade wanted to know.

"No, it's out in the trash. That reminds me, I need to sign up for a trash service." She wrote a note and stuck it on the refrigerator before returning to the table.

Levi grabbed a pastry then asked, "What else? Reed already told us about your garden."

From his scowl, she guessed Levi wasn't in the mood to forgive her yet. "So you know he replanted everything as a surprise for me." Lily rather enjoyed sticking up for him for a change.

"What else, Lily?" Reed nailed her with a glacial tone and look that told her he wasn't ready to let her off the hook yet, either.

Mentioning the misplaced DVDs would embarrass her in front of so many people, especially since she assumed Reed's brothers weren't aware of her organized collection. "You'll think I'm nuts," she said instead.

Her brother scoffed. "I already do, so what else?"

She fidgeted under the stern stares of the two men who meant the most to her then just said it. "Several of my movies were out of order on the shelves."

Her brother explained, "Lily is meticulous about her mystery collections, and anal when it comes to keeping them in alphabetical order. If any were out of place, she didn't do it."

"I can vouch for that." Reed grasped her hand. "Someone's been in your house. You have a secure dead bolt now, but that didn't stop him from destroying your garden or SUV."

Reed's words sent an icy shiver trickling down Lily's spine. Who had it out for her, and, even more puzzling, why?

"Slade and I will dig out that wiring and get going," Brett said a few minutes later. "Lily, if you think of anyone or anything we can look into, don't hesitate to tell Reed. Even a trivial altercation could trigger a disturbed person into violence."

Reed saw the flashing lights and tow truck out the window and squeezed Lily's hand before standing. "I'll help you after I speak to the tow service."

"When did you call them?"

Wondering at the hint of accusation in her tone and flash of annoyance in her eyes, he replied, "Before we came in. This will just take a minute."

"I'll come with you," Levi insisted.

Reed shrugged, figuring Lily's brother was as protective of her as he. At least Levi waited until his brothers drove off and he dealt with the tow service before rounding on him.

"I'm not happy Lily's taken up with a Kincaid," Levi stated bluntly.

With worry for Lily's safety uppermost in his mind and her safety his top priority, he wasn't going to mince words with Levi. "I'll say this once. Neither I nor my brothers are our father, so don't judge us by his lifestyle. I care deeply for Lily. You can trust me with her welfare, as I don't plan to leave her side until this threat is stopped."

"I'll keep you company with that," Levi insisted.

Smiling, he drawled, "Do you honestly believe your sister will go for that? She's going to balk at having me shadow her."

The tension went out of Levi's rigid shoulders, the stern tightness to his mouth releasing in a rueful grin. "No. If she digs her heels in, she can turn stubborn."

"Our girl possesses many admirable traits. Allowing me, or anyone else to keep such close tabs on her isn't one of them."

Cocking his head, Levi glanced at him with a measure of respect, easing Reed's own tension in regards to getting along with Lily's brother. "I might grow to like you, Kincaid. Let's deal with my sister together."

He'd expected to find Lily nervous or upset about learning she had a stalker, but instead, she was wiping down the kitchen with angry, jerky arm swipes across the countertops, frustration pouring off her in waves.

"Time to talk," Levi said when she ignored them.

"Nothing to discuss right now, is there?" She faced them with a piqued look. "Someone doesn't like me. We have no idea who, and no way to learn who until we catch them. You and Vickie can go home now."

Her brother could deal with her first, he decided. She wasn't in the mood to be flexible.

"Not unless you agree to certain safety precautions," Levi insisted, his hands on his hips.

Reed leaned against a counter and watched her toss the washcloth in the sink, cast him a quick look then face her brother with a frown. "I'm not stupid. I won't go anywhere alone. Trina's with me at work. If I'm there alone during lunch, I always lock the door." She spread her arms. "What else can I do?"

"I can work from here and offered to stay, but she refused." Vickie looked worried and disappointed.

"No need, I'll be staying here and following her

to work." Reed went to Lily and drew her against him. "This won't last long before we find out who's behind these attacks, I promise."

"You sound sure of yourself. I like that."

Lily pulled away enough to send Levi an amused glance. "You like something about the guy I'm seeing? There's hope for you yet, Levi."

"He gets brownie points for replanting your garden for you." He glared at Reed. "We'll go, but I want daily reports."

"Not a problem." Reed ignored Lily's annoyed huff.

"It was a long drive for a short stay, but now I'm glad we made it," Vickie told Lily as they walked out to the car, the absence of Lily's damaged vehicle a noticeable reminder of why they had made the impromptu visit. "I shouldn't have promised not to tell Levi about the mugging."

"I shouldn't have put you in that position." Lily hugged her and then Levi, and Reed could tell how close the siblings were. "Talk to you soon. I'll drive down to Cheyenne my next weekend free of bookings."

"You do that." Levi turned to Reed with his hand out. "Take care of her or you'll answer to me."

"You got it."

Lily nudged him and glared at her brother. "Knock it off."

Reed waited until Lily got busy in the kitchen again before bringing up his opinion on who might have it in for her. She stood at the sink rinsing out the coffeepot and he carried over the last two cups.

"I'm sorry to bring up a bad subject, but we should consider your stalker might be one of John's disgruntled exes."

Lily paused, that possibility having never occurred to her. Between the shock of waking up to her damaged property then dealing with Levi's unexpected visit and anger, she couldn't think straight, let alone come up with a possible culprit. As far as she was aware, none of John's affairs had lasted beyond a few hookups. *It's a meaningless, harmless release. I don't promise anything beyond that, and make sure she's of the same mind. It has no impact on my feelings for you.* Those lines were his favorite comeback when she stopped believing his stories and lies.

"Whoever they were, the affair meant as little to them as they did to John. He said so himself those last few months before I gave up and left." She tensed again, remembering the months of arguing and wasted efforts, another unwelcome distraction.

Reed brushed his fingers down her arm, the light touch both soothing and a warning she wouldn't like what he said next. "And he always told you the truth?"

Lily closed her eyes against the stab of pain she hadn't experienced since seeing Pam again resurrected that hurtful last fight with John. She shifted away from Reed, the hurt from that reminder slowly changing to annoyance. "You know he didn't," she returned, miffed he would say that.

Grabbing the damp cloth, she swiped over the counter and around the sink, rubbing harder the longer she considered the idea one of John's bimbo's might harbor a grudge against her, for whatever perverted reason. If not one of them, then some other deranged individual whom she happened to catch the eye of. Lucky her, she thought sarcastically.

"Lily."

Reed reached a hand out to her as she stepped over to the island and took her growing anger out on that countertop. Ignoring him, she continued cleaning, dwelling on her bad luck or inability to shake the mistake of her marriage, whichever turned out to be the case. Her irritation morphed into anger as she thought about the injustice of being targeted when she'd done nothing to deserve such treatment. Instead of the blues pulling her down when she thought about the futility of trying to save a worthless marriage, a red haze of fury filled her head and made her dizzy. She scrubbed cabinet sides for no other reason than to keep from lashing out, recalling the wasted time and energy that had dragged her down for so long. She hadn't felt this helpless frenzy consuming her body and mind since right after her parents died, and she didn't have a clue how to deal with the anger overload any better now. She always aided others in bad situations, not the other way around.

Reed tried to clasp her hand, but she jerked away and strode to the table, snapping back at him. "Leave me alone."

"Not going to happen, so deal with it, and me."

His rough implacable tone ground against her frayed nerves, fueling her outrage until it spread throughout her body, tensing every muscle, cramping every joint. The efforts to hold onto something that was never there to begin with brought tears to her eyes, blurring her vision, which added to her escalating fury. Her usual mild-mannered, composed, compassionate self deserted her, and she let loose with an uncontrollable swipe across the table, sending the two bakery boxes filled with trash to the floor.

Lily rounded on Reed, glaring, her body vibrating with uncontrollable emotional overload. "Don't dictate to me. I listened to John tell me to deal with what he called my *insecurities* for way too long, and I don't want consoling, or calm gestures, or meaningless words. I've had enough of that crap to last a lifetime." Ignoring his glacial, narrow-eyed gaze, she started to pace, waving the damp cloth around as she continued to rant. "I can't believe one of his bimbos is targeting me. I left him, they were welcome to him, and that was over a year-and-a-half ago, so why now? And why would some psycho come after me? I'm a nobody…" The scratchiness of his calloused hand shackling her wrist halted her tirade but not her automatic response of raising her other arm to retaliate.

Reed moved fast, halted her swing by gripping that wrist, leaving her panting, facing his wrath, shocked at her behavior, yet not sorry. He yanked her against him, his tone rough as he said, "You want to play rough, Lily? I have a better way for you to release your anger."

The roaring in her head muted his words but not the rumble of his chest against hers, or the outline of his rigid cock grinding against her mound. His dark, commanding tone tugged at her nipples, had her sheath going damp with a different kind of heat that spread to envelop her whole body. He didn't wait for an answer before spinning her around and nudging her over the table, releasing her wrists to brace on her forearms before he pushed her shorts down.

Lily groaned, everything else forgotten as sheer lust took over her senses. She still shook from her volatile outburst, hungering for an outlet to vent her roiling, contradictive emotions. He always knew what she needed before she did, sliding two fingers inside her with a deep plunge that rasped sensitive tissues already inflamed with arousal. His name slipped past her constricted throat on a breathy moan. "Reed." It seemed whenever he took her over, that was all she could think of to say, just his name, just him.

"I'm here, Lily. Remember that." A sharp, stinging slap covered one buttock, and she went up on her toes with an embracing whimper, loving the distracting hot throb. "Feel free to come at me with all you've got, but remember how I retaliate."

Reed spread his fingers inside her, stretching the tight muscles then pulling out with a scrape over her clit. She thrust against his palm resting against the center of her cheeks, craving more. "Don't stop," she demanded, desperate for his mind-fogging possession. "And don't wait."

"Damn it," he swore, using one booted foot to spread her legs farther. "Don't regret this."

"I won't," she stated with surety, hearing him lower his zipper. His cock bounced off her butt, the tap both odd and titillating. Her pulse quickened, her pussy rippling as he removed his fingers and latched onto her hips.

"Grab hold of the table," he instructed, tunneling his way inside her with his sheathed cock.

Lily stretched her arms, grasping the table edge, and laid her forehead down, gasping at his full penetration. She squeezed around his welcome girth, trembling from the immediate onslaught of pleasure, his pummeling deep thrusts aimed to abrade her tender clit. The small kitchen echoed with his grunts, her labored breathing, the slap of his hips against her buttocks and his groin against her seeping vagina.

"Fuck, but you're tight, and so damn responsive."

She would respond but her breath lodged in her throat, trapped so she couldn't breathe except for ragged gasps. Instead, she arched with each plunge and lifted her hips with each withdrawal until he tightened his hold, sliding one thumb between her cheeks to press inside her back orifice. Lily's startled gasp ended on a moan, the onslaught of new sensations hitting her with a suffusion of blistering hot, heightened arousal. *"Reed!"* she cried out, her pussy convulsing, rippling around his rock-hard erection.

"Let go, Lily," he insisted, his voice hoarse. "I've got you."

Unable to do anything except lie there and endure the hot licks of pleasure taking over her body, Lily rode the tempest until she went mindless with the sensations engulfing her mind and body.

Chapter Twelve

Reed pulled his phone out, answering Slade's call with, "What's up?" while waiting for Lily to finish dressing for work. Neither one of them had slept much over the weekend. He'd continued to probe her memory for anyone who might hold a grudge against her, making them both testy. She swore there was nobody, but she trusted the homeless on sight instead of learning their circumstances first, proving her gullibility. Unsavory characters lurked downtown among those innocent of wrongdoing, but Lily refused to turn her back on anyone who appeared to need help. It was one of the traits he admired most about her and now worried him the most.

"Lily's wiring was frayed with a knife."

His brother's blunt words formed a tight knot in his gut. "The electrician agreed with you, then?" Slade had mentioned the possibility yesterday, after examining the wires with a magnifying glass and making comparisons with enlarged photos of old, damaged wiring.

"Yep. Just spoke to him. Did she give you anything to go on yet?"

Slade's frustration and concern came through loud and clear. "No, other than she believes the mugging and the vandalism at her house aren't related. She still thinks the attack was random."

"Brett and I don't believe so."

"Neither do I, and I wouldn't chance her welfare either way."

Which was what Reed had told Lily after he'd calmed her down with sex following her meltdown. He'd seen her sweet, compassionate, sad, and happy, but Lily in a full-blown rage was a sight to behold and one he wouldn't forget. He preferred not to witness another if it stemmed from a threat to her safety or a reminder of her painful past.

"We're here to help," Slade said, interrupting his thoughts.

Reed couldn't resist needling him. "Aren't you always saying you don't want to get involved?"

"She's yours, so I'm involved," he returned without pause.

"Yes, she is," he murmured, Slade's words a simple declaration of their close bond, his brother's unconditional support easing his worry. Lily entered the kitchen looking summery in a yellow, sleeveless dress with bright pink flowers. She'd been hiding her anxiety behind a calm demeanor since her blowup Saturday, but he'd seen through that same stoic façade she'd presented during rough patches since first witnessing the tension between her with John. "I'll catch up with you at the ranch shortly." He hung up and handed her a travel mug. "Ready?"

"Yes, and I'll say it once more. There's no reason for you to take up a chunk of your morning following me to work. No one will harass me on the road with so much traffic. Plus, I'll be in a different vehicle."

He picked up his Stetson on their way out, double checking the lock after closing the door. "I'll feel better, and you were adamant about having your car today instead of letting me drive you. Call me if Trina leaves for lunch, and don't unlock the doors if you're there alone while she's gone," he told her, leading her to the rental parked next to his truck. Opening the car door, he grinned at her eye roll. "Humor me."

"Fine. I'm not dumb, you know. I'm plenty scared enough to be extra careful and keep an eye out for anyone suspicious hanging around." Lily settled behind the wheel and shifted on the seat. "I miss my

Mazda. This feels like I'm sitting on the ground."

"You're accustomed to the higher SUV. I'm the same with the truck. You'll get used to it, though, and it's temporary. Again, you're the one who insisted on taking separate cars."

"With good reason. I don't want to impose on Trina if you are delayed or can't make it. This way, we're covering all contingencies."

Reed understood her reluctance to cede all independence and rely solely on someone else. "Drive carefully," was all he said before closing the door. The extra drive did cut into his morning but was worth the price to lessen his anxiety.

There was safety in numbers, he kept repeating all the way to Creative Events, and between working with Trina and seeing clients, she wouldn't be alone. That logic worked out in his head, which didn't explain the hard thud of his heartbeat when he told her goodbye.

"Go, Reed," Trina insisted when he lingered inside the building. "I promise I won't leave her alone."

Lily went up on her toes to kiss him then shoved him toward the door. "I have work to do, and so do you. Goodbye."

"I'll be here by four thirty." Returning to his

truck, Reed didn't glance around despite the ball of dread cramping his abdomen.

****

"I imagine he's a nice change for you," Trina said, locking the door behind Reed.

"He's definitely a change, I'll say that." Lily tossed her purse on the desk and sat down, already tired of the precautions and feeling guilty for imposing so much on Reed. She agreed with the necessity. She just didn't like the burden her troubles were putting on everyone.

Trina picked up her cup off the desk and padded over to the coffee bar, talking over her shoulder. "C'mon. Admit he's special, at least to me. Before this shit all came down, I never saw you so happy. The Kincaids are good people."

"They are, but the overprotectiveness takes getting used to. Before Reed, Levi was the only person who cared enough to both hover and browbeat at the same time. It's the reason for it now that's grating on my nerves."

Except when he'd exerted his dominance to calm her down from her uncharacteristic tirade. She would accept that kind of protectiveness anytime, anywhere. The things he could make her feel, the depth of her craving for more of him, still shook her. Lust, love, or a combination of both? That was a question she kept putting off answering, unsure if she was ready to face the truth. She booted up the computer, determined to work until Trina handed her a coffee refill and asked the one question she didn't have an answer for yet.

"You can't think of anyone who would do such things to you?"

"No one," she replied, shaking her head. "Thanks. I have today's schedule up. Our last appointment is at two unless we get a walk-in or call. This morning is booked, starting in fifteen minutes."

Taking her seat, Trina nodded, scanned something Lily couldn't see then lifted her gaze, frowning. "Looking at the weekend reminded me of the Davidson cancellation. Given your falling out, have you considered she's your antagonist? You told me you first saw her again at the charity and right after, you were attacked."

"Pam?" Lily shook her head then thought back, recalling Delia mentioning Pam's searing glare behind Lily's back at the farmer's market, probably the same scorn she'd given her when they met out front last week. Even so, she couldn't picture Pam retaliating against her after her heartfelt remorse for sleeping with John. "I doubt it. The friend I once knew so well would never commit such acts, and I can't believe she's changed that much."

"I'll bet, at one time, you wouldn't have believed she could sleep with your husband, either." A car pulled in out front, likely their client, and Trina said, "Something to consider."

Trina struck a nerve with that comment, and Lily was grateful for the busy morning that kept her from dwelling on the possibility that Pam was the one tormenting her. It took a deranged mind to plan and execute most of what she'd gone through. Pam might have switched from remorseful to angry when Lily refused to rekindle their friendship, but she wasn't off her rocker. Then again, she'd spent over a year convincing herself John loved her enough to change, proving she was a lousy judge of character.

After their last morning client left, they discussed lunch, and Trina called in an order for delivery while Lily took a call from Delia. They hadn't spoken in a while with Lily spending so much time with Reed lately, and guilt nudged her into answering instead of putting Delia off until she was safe.

"Hi there. How are you?"

"I'm good and have a rare day off. How about

lunch?" Delia asked, the hopeful lilt in her voice adding to Lily's guilt.

"I'd like to but can't. Reed and his brothers think the mugging is connected to some vandalism at my house and that I've got some whack job hassling me." Delia knew about the mugging, but there had been no reason to mention anything else until now.

"That's awful! And scary. Are you okay?"

"Other than spooked, yes. I plan to stay here when not with Reed. Rain check?"

Delia's concern changed to peevish exasperation. "He doesn't trust *me*? Tell him to take a hike - that's offensive."

Lily bristled at her tone, not in the mood to cater to Delia's insecurities. "At least he's concerned about my welfare," she returned, her cool tone drawing Trina's frowning glance.

"I'm sorry, Lily. I had a bad weekend and didn't mean to take it out on you. Is there anything I can do?"

Her remorse sounded genuine, and Lily didn't hold grudges. "No, thanks for asking. Reed plans on staying at my place for now. Between him and his brothers, they'll find some clue to this person's identity before long." She had to believe that or go nuts.

"I don't doubt it, so I won't worry too much. Keep in touch if you can."

Lily said goodbye, adding another benefit to getting involved with Reed, an excuse to hang out with Delia less. She didn't have enough spare time for such a clingy, needy friend. Her thoughts had turned to another friend during the afternoon, and she couldn't shake Trina's suggestion to consider Pam her nemesis. She hated to believe her once best friend would retaliate against her in such ways. Just the same, she would talk to Reed tonight and get his opinion.

Reed didn't draw a steady breath until he saw Lily again that afternoon, his tension loosening the moment she walked out of Creative Events wearing a smile. Tonight, he would ask her to show him any of John's belongings she'd kept, including paperwork. John was closemouthed about his affairs before taking up with Lily, and even more so when he started cheating on her a year into their marriage. The only thing he let slip during one of their arguments was he met his dates at their places, or a hotel, never in public. If she kept them, charge card receipts for those hotels would give them somewhere to start asking around.

He broached the subject over dinner, reaching across the table to pour her another glass of wine. "We need to discuss how to find this person. I have an idea where to start, but it will be painful for you."

Lily sipped her wine, her eyes steady on him as she set the glass down. "I'm over John and our marriage, Reed." She flashed one of her impetuous grins. "I'm into you, now. What do you need?"

That was as close as she'd come to admitting her feelings, enough to set his pulse racing as he imagined their future together. First things first, however. "John's charge card receipts. Did you keep any?"

"I have all of that in storage, along with some furniture I couldn't fit here. You want to look for hotel charges then question the employees. That makes more sense than Trina's suggestion."

He listened while she told him about her best friend from college, displeased he was just now hearing about her. "You should have mentioned her sooner. What's important to you, like getting mugged, is important to me." Rising, he reached for her plate but paused when she placed a hand on his wrist.

"Most of that went on before anything serious developed between us."

"You're right," he admitted, his annoyance slipping away. "We're both on edge. Let's take the wine to the couch and watch a movie. We'll pick up those files tomorrow."

The person harboring a deep hatred for Lily waited on the corner until all the lights went out in her house. Catching her alone was impossible with her fucking bodyguard or someone else always around. Venting on her vehicle did nothing to lessen the rage, and playtime was over. After waiting another twenty minutes, the black-clad figure lifted the gasoline can from the back seat and crept behind the houses toward the oblivious couple. Taking Kincaid out, too, was icing on the cake, a delicious way to end this. There was a certain amount of satisfaction just from dousing her precious gardens around the house Lily loved so much. The flames engulfing their screams would be worth the long wait and hassle.

Reed didn't know what woke him, likely a sixth sense from living on a ranch where any number of late-night sounds could rouse him from sleep. He lay there a moment, an arm wrapped around Lily, not wanting to move until a shadow crossed the window. A cold wave of apprehension spread through his body. Tightening his arm in warning, he pressed his mouth to her ear. "Lily, wake up... *shhh*," he whispered when she groaned. "Someone is outside. Don't turn on the light but call 911. Stay here until I get back."

He didn't wait for an answer, sliding out of bed, he crouched down to pull on jeans and grab his gun. Staying low, he made his way to the front door and checked outside before closing it behind him, furious at the injustice of someone terrorizing Lily. This ended tonight, one way or another, he swore, his attention caught by mumbling from around the side of the house. The light next to the door spread a meager glow toward the end of the porch, enough for him to move with stealth and speed without tripping in the dark. The pungent odor of gasoline hit him before he even reached the corner, sending his adrenaline into overdrive.

Screw sneaking up on the bastard. He wouldn't risk Lily's safety to take this guy by surprise. Whipping around the corner, gun raised and aimed, he saw a small person covered in a black hooded robe holding a gasoline can. Reed tightened his hand on the gun, doing his best to ignore the lust for vengeance that demanded a quick, permanent end to this by simply pulling the trigger.

"Don't fucking move," he ordered with no time to wait for help to arrive. "Trust me, I'll use this, so drop the can and come here."

"I don't think so." The feminine voice didn't surprise him, but her gall did when she set the can down but didn't budge. "You think you're going to save that bitch? Think again," she stated with contempt. Holding up a lighter, she flicked it open, the small flame enough to sicken him with fear for Lily.

Cocking the gun hammer, he gave her one more chance. "Close it, or I shoot. I won't warn you again."

She jumped away from the garden bed, tossing the lighter, her manic, cackling laughter revealing the depth of her depraved, unhinged mind. "Me or your precious Lily. You choose," she taunted.

Bile filled his throat as the flames spread up the side of the house and traveled toward the rear, where he guessed she'd started spreading the gasoline. With no time to spare or think, he took a shot then tore toward the front, the woman's sharp cry of pain echoing in the night air. His heart damn near pounded through his chest as he burst through the door, the house already reeking of smoke. "Lily!" he yelled, dashing inside in frantic haste only to come to an abrupt halt when she flew against him wrapped in a blanket. "That's my girl," he praised her, light-headed with relief. Picking her up, he hightailed it back outside.

Lily coughed, squeezing him until he couldn't breathe, yet she managed to ask, "Did...did you...catch him?"

"Her, and she's wounded." Breathing heavily, Reed set her down on the lawn, hearing sirens seconds before seeing flashing lights and neighbors emerging from their homes.

Hugging the blanket with one hand, she laid the other on his arm, fingers trembling against his quivering muscles. "Go find her. I'm fine."

In that moment, with her house going up in flames and nothing but grim resolve etched on her pale face, nothing could stop him from telling her what had been in his heart for years. "I love you." Hauling her against him, he kissed her then took off, reached the backyard, and glimpsed the woman's hobbling retreat behind the neighbor's house.

Lily leaned against the police car, eyeing her burning house with stunned disbelief and a slow churning anger. It wasn't the physical structure she cared so much about but the threatening risk to Reed. A fine mist from the firehoses sprayed her face, cooling her skin and clearing her head of the lingering fear. She had still been on the phone with 911 when she smelled smoke, her window glowing with the flames already licking around the glass pane, her first concern for Reed. Frantic to check on him and get to safety, she'd snatched the blanket and run, his voice adding to the watery sheen filling her eyes.

"Here, drink this."

She took the bottled water from the cop, smiling in gratitude. "Thank you."

He nodded, gazing at the fire-engulfed house. "Any idea what happened?"

"Not what, who," she answered. *Pam.* That was who popped into her head the moment Reed corrected her with *she*.

"Arson?" He cast her a skeptical look. "Are you sure? These older homes can have faulty wiring, or maybe it was a gas leak. We don't have crimes like arson here in Eagle's Nest."

"Tell that to them." Lily nodded toward Reed escorting a limping hooded figure across the lawn, breathing easier with his safe return. The woman lifted her head, the hood falling down, her identity another body-slamming shock.

"Delia?"

Reed signaled the paramedic before dragging

Delia in front of Lily. "You two know each other, I presume."

"How could you?" she choked out, shaking her head in disbelief. "What did I ever do to you?"

Delia yanked against Reed's hold, trying to get in her face and failing. "If not for you, I would be with John now. He loved me, not you, but you refused to leave. Your delay cost me everything: the love of my life, his love for me."

Delia and John? It shouldn't surprise her, but, after all of Delia's friendly overtures, it did. Thinking of her duplicity, plotting, and attacks, Lily set aside her sympathy for the blunt truth. "John didn't love anyone except himself. I'm sorry you didn't see that, but why take it out on me after I filed for divorce?"

"Exactly what I was thinking." Reed glared at Delia then released her to the paramedics. "Keep talking," he instructed. "It's only a flesh wound."

"He changed," she snapped, fighting the paramedics until Reed helped them secure her on the gurney. Struggling against the leather straps on her wrists and ankles, she screeched, "He didn't want me anymore, said he wanted to be alone after all you put him through." Delia didn't stop ranting even while they checked her wound. "I refused to let him deny our love, and gave him one more chance, only he was too pigheaded to take it."

Delia snickered, the pure manic evil sending a shiver down Lily's spine. Nausea churned in her abdomen remembering all the time she'd spent alone with someone she never really knew.

"You need help, Delia. Maybe a shrink can get through your delusions."

"You think I'm delusional? Not so much that I got away with killing the son of a bitch."

"Get her out of here," Reed commanded, wrapping an arm around Lily's rigid shoulders.

Lily shifted her gaze away from Delia's red, angry face, leaning against Reed. "Tell me it's over." She glanced up at him, needing his reassurance, wondering if there were any more sucker punches she'd have to endure tonight. Unlike her, he didn't appear surprised by Delia's last admission.

She followed the slow turn of his head as he took in the police, firemen, and neighbors

who'd heard Delia's deranged ranting and confession. "It's over."

"Thank God because I love you, too, and I couldn't bear..." A sob escaped her and she sagged against him. "C-couldn't stand it if..." He drew her close and she crumpled, his strength a soothing balm against her battered soul.

Reed guided Lily to his truck parked at the curb, shaking his head at the people who started to come forward with offers of help. He would take care of her, starting by enclosing them in the cab so she could let it out then calm down in privacy. Keeping her close, he looked at the destruction of her beloved home as the siren-wailing ambulance carrying the woman responsible drove past them. The woman Lily called Delia would end up in a psych hospital, which was where she needed to be, as long as it was for life. He didn't doubt he would have the backing of the entire highway patrol and state police to ensure that sentence. A heavy weight pressed on his chest, thinking of John and eyeing the blackened ruin of Lily's house while her tears dampened his chest. So much waste and heartache.

He found his phone and called his brothers. A long night loomed ahead for both of them.

****

Two days later

Lily halted pacing in front of the wide glass doors in Reed's great room when she heard vehicles out front. The afternoon had crept by waiting for Reed, his brothers, and Levi to return from Casper and their meeting with the prosecutor in charge of Delia's case. "Finally," she said, hungry for both the outcome of Delia's fate and dinner.

"Much longer and you would have worn the stain off Reed's beautiful wood floor."

"He wouldn't mind," she told Vickie. Lily didn't try to persuade Levi and Vickie not to drive up yesterday. She wanted them here as much as they had needed to come, and there was room enough in Reed's home for a dozen guests.

Allie nodded from her seat on the leather sofa. "I can verify that. Let's hope today put an end to that crazy woman's freedom."

"It did," Reed stated, entering the room and striding toward Lily.

Relief washed through her in a warm rush, loosening every muscle, Reed's confidence rubbing off on her. She was done suffering from John's mistakes and poor judgment, more than ready to embrace a future with Reed. Her only regret now was the time it took to see he was perfect for her.

"What did you learn?" she asked when Levi, Brett, and Slade joined them.

The day after she lost her house, Reed ran up to the mercantile and purchased a pair of jeans and a shirt so Lily could wear something besides the sleep shirt and shorts she'd hurried into before escaping her smoke-filled house. Lily had spent six hours with the police the previous afternoon, rehashing every conversation and get-together with Delia that she could recall. Between Reed's constant presence and the overwhelming support from law enforcement, she got through that and the loss of her home with relative calm. What a difference it made having someone who really cared at her side through the rough times, someone who knew when she needed his dominant control and when a hug would work better at settling her emotions.

"She's going to an institution for the criminally insane," Reed answered, leaning down to brush his lips over hers. "She won't get out, so you can forget all about her."

Brett strolled over to the bar, saying, "According to her, she intended to kill you the night she came at you with a bat, but the security guard arrived sooner than she'd expected Then she got a perverse kick out of befriending you, learning when you would be away from the house to break in through the bathroom window, which she left rigged not to lock when you invited her over."

Lily had never considered the smaller window

in the bathroom as a possible entry until Reed insisted she put on a dead bolt. That's what she got for believing small towns were safer than big cities. "She was so devious, and I never saw it."

"No one did, including John." Sadness colored Reed's voice. "She bragged how easy it was to crush the entire refill of his sleep meds and mix them with the alcohol. The drugs were in the coroner's report, but, with no proof of foul play and the combination an often-used suicide option, he signed off on it."

"And John never knew what hit him." Lily viewed that as a blessing.

Levi crossed over to her and brushed his knuckles under her chin, a gesture he often did when she was a teen and down about their parents' deaths. "Served him right for his behavior, if you ask me."

"She's sick, Levi, and you're biased," Lily returned, which he ignored with a *what if I am* shrug.

"A raving lunatic." Slade kissed the top of her head. "No one but her to blame." He took the whiskey Brett handed him and let out an exaggerated sigh. "I suppose, now that Reed's attached at the hip like big brother, Mom will nag me even more. Thanks a lot, guys."

She pulled away from Reed to give Slade a hug, giggling as she tossed his words back at him. "No one to blame except yourself."

"Besides," Reed stated, yanking her next to him again, "you might like settling down as much as we do. It just takes the right woman."

"There isn't one," he insisted.

Allie and Lily answered at the same time. "Yes, there is."

She watched Levi clasp Vickie's hand then gazed at Reed, who gave her one of those powerful, heady looks that curled her toes and inflamed her senses. "There's someone for everyone."

"Damn straight. Took you long enough."

Too long. With that thought in mind, she whispered, "I'll make it up to you starting after dinner. I need to get hold of someone then I'll join you in the kitchen. Casseroles are warm in the oven."

"I'll hold you to that." Reed tugged her braid and nipped her lower lip before following the others to the kitchen.

With her scalp throbbing and her lip tingling, Lily retrieved her phone from her purse and typed a short text, hoping this would put the past to rest once and for all.

Hey, Pam. If you're still interested, I can make

time to meet for lunch next week.

Chapter Thirteen

When Reed arrived at Casey's three weeks later, Lily was more than ready for her first exposure to one of their play parties. Under the light cotton slip-on dress she wore, the soft fabric of the ruffle-trimmed camisole and short set he'd surprised her with teased her bare skin. She'd never gone out in public without underwear, and, when he removed the dress, the soft drape of the camisole would cling to the nipple huggers causing her tips to throb in a pleasant, arousing pulse. Living with him offered a lot more opportunity for Reed to demonstrate just how submissive she was to his dominant sexual control, and the creative ways he could show her all she'd been missing. The nipple stimulants were new, effective enough to dampen her shorts and keep her on edge with needy anticipation.

Reed had been there for her every step of the way during the days following Delia's attack and the loss of her house. She couldn't have gotten through the blur of activity and coping with the constant topsy-turvy ride of emotional disruptions without him and her family, and friends. Levi and Vickie's week-long stay and support helped with that first week of deciding what to do with the lot after signing off on having the charred structure torn down and the debris cleared. Donating it for a neighborhood playground brought her joy instead of sorrow whenever she stopped by to watch the progress. The neighbors were enthusiastic with their gratitude, the kids asking repeatedly when they could jump on the in-ground trampoline, climb on the large jungle gym, or go down the winding tube slide.

Trina hadn't hesitated to free her from work obligations without a time limit, but Lily needed the distraction after her brother left, so she pushed Reed out the door to attend to his own neglected work. Living with him doubled her driving time into Casper, so they came up with a schedule that allowed Lily to work from home three days a week. Taking advantage of the new schedule, she'd met Pam for lunch the other day, and, although awkward at first, they managed to talk their way past bitter feelings and start the process of becoming friends again. After suspecting her of such horrible retaliation, Pam's fervent willingness to reconcile expunged

Lily's guilt.

Reed parked in front of Casey's, and her heart turned over watching him come around the truck to her side. Of all the support pouring out for her these past weeks, nothing meant as much as his arms coming around her every night and rough whispers of love mixed with titillating, erotic hints of what he planned to do to her. Waking to his snug hold each morning, and, sometimes an arousing butt swat to get her motivated, started her day humming with expectation – a welcome change from the days of fretting about unexplained bad luck.

Taking Reed's hand, she hopped down and took in the fewer-than-usual vehicles in the parking lot, recognizing Brett and Slade's trucks. "Will this be all, then?" She had questioned whether his definition of a small gathering was the same as hers and, assuming two or more people arrived in each vehicle, she had slightly underestimated the number.

"Maybe one or two more. There were a couple of maybes for tonight, and I don't see their cars," he replied, leading her to the stairs. "Weeknights are difficult for some who have kids or other obligations."

"I still say Jordon and Bianca shouldn't have postponed their engagement party. We could have attended the one planned that week."

The thoughtful gesture from a couple Lily didn't know all that well was one reason she entered the private space without jitters even though others were present tonight. The calls of concern from Reed's friends she'd never met revealed the bond the group shared, and her goal tonight was to make him proud while testing her submissive limits.

Reed closed the door, turned his back to the room, and reached for the hem of her simple summer sheath. "Set the guilt aside, Lily, and concentrate on having fun. No one minded the delay."

Drawing the garment over her head, he left her standing in the soft knit rose lingerie set, the luxurious material caressing her bare skin providing no barrier to the arousing scrape of his nail across one pointed nipple. Without conscious thought, Lily leaned into him, proof how easy and rewarding she found succumbing to his every touch.

"Well, since you're in Dom mode, I'll have to, won't I?" she teased, brushing her lips over his neck.

He brushed her shorter hair over her shoulder, the six inches she'd had cut off a final goodbye to the past. "Have I ever mentioned I love how quickly you catch on?"

Lily grinned and took his hand, conscious of the obvious sway of her breasts and adorned nipples as they walked toward the corner bar. Some of her self-consciousness slipped away with her first look at the apparatus in use and the various outfits the women wore. Or not, she mused, stumbling slightly when Jordon waved them over to the sofa where Bianca cuddled naked on his lap. Luckily, Bianca's lack of modesty made it less uncomfortable to converse with the couple.

In a move so casual it was hardly noticeable, Jordon glided his knuckles under Bianca's breasts, raising a brow. "Why is it either you or Slade is always the last to arrive? I figured now that you're committed, that would change."

"This time, a downed steer delayed me, but we're here now and looking forward to your fall wedding," Reed replied.

"Brett and Allie first, though, and coming soon," Bianca said, shifting as Jordon toyed with one nipple then gazing at Lily. "She's so excited about your ideas. I can't wait for you and Trina to start on ours."

"We're already coming up with suggestions for you. October weddings open up all kinds of options that differ from summer." Reed sighed, drawing Lily's attention. "What? Too much girl talk?"

"Yes," Reed and Jordon responded together,

Jordon sliding his hand down to graze Bianca's bare labia with his fingers. They shared a look Lily envied, hers soft and accepting of his public fondling, his proud in a way she ached to see reflected on Reed's face.

Without a word, Reed continued on, and as they strolled by the St. Andrew's cross, she took in the bound woman and her leather-strap-wielding partner with blood-pumping interest. Lily's cheeks clenched watching the Dom strike her white buttocks with the strap, imagining the heat and sting the red slash produced.

Reed steered her forward, running a hand across her buttocks. "I can start out much lighter."

Her mouth went dry, imagining the heightened burn a strap could yield. "I'll think about it," was all she could manage to say.

From hidden speakers, a sultry female voice provided extra stimulus with a tune Lily didn't recognize but that stirred her senses, along with the electrically charged scenes and the tantalizing glide of her clothing. By the time they reached the bar, her need to prove to him she wanted to fit into this part of his life was as strong as her continued craving for his possession. Slade manned the bar, her nipples hard and prominent enough to draw his gaze before he handed her a rum and Coke with a wink, dispelling the awkward moment.

"Thanks." Lily sipped, the cold carbonated alcohol relieving her parched throat.

"I didn't see Deb," Reed said, picking up his beer.

Slade shrugged. "Not tonight."

Curious, Lily glanced from Reed to his brother. "I didn't know you were with someone."

"I'm not, at least, not like you're thinking."

Reed leaned against a stool, spread his knees, and pulled her between them. "Slade doesn't date or stick with one play partner, and Deb, whom you haven't met, is of the same mind. It works for them, for now."

She smiled at his emphasis on "for now'" and Slade's frown. "Reed changed my thinking on giving another relationship a try, Slade. You never know what, or who tomorrow will bring."

Ignoring her, he addressed Reed. "Speaking of which, I heard today the Studman place sold, the new owner planning to start an animal rescue."

"Ten acres is enough space, depending on how many and as long as they're domestic, not wild animals since that property is right between our ranch and Bailey's spread."

Lily listened with half an ear, sipping her drink until she spotted Allie and Brett emerging from the office room in the hall. A longing swept through her as she glimpsed
Brett's indulgent look at Allie's contented expression, a strong desire for her and Reed to become that close and comfortable here, to see him that proud of her. Allie accepted the water bottle Slade handed over, appearing at ease in front of everyone with her nipples protruding from the holes in her lacy bra and her thong clinging to her damp folds. Lily wondered how long it had taken her to feel that comfortable in front of her future brothers-in-law.

Brett nodded his thanks for the beer then asked Reed, "Did we lose the steer?"

"No, just a sprain. He's in the barn for a while, not happy."

"No doubt," Brett returned with a wry look.

Allie rested against his side, smiling at Lily. "What do you think of your first gathering?"

"There's a lot to take in, but I'm enjoying myself." *And hoping I find the guts to show Reed how much he means to me.*

Reed tightened his arm around her waist. "Let me know if you have a preference on trying anything,

Lily."

A delicate tremor went through her, Reed's rough timbre affecting her as strongly as deciding her preference was to please him. Before she lost her nerve, she scanned the room, pointed, and whispered, "Can we go to that corner?"

His answer was to give her a squeeze and address his brothers. "Excuse us." Pressing her lower back, he drew her to the oversized stuffed chair in the corner where he sat down and placed his hands on her hips. "You're used to me making these decisions, but given this is your first public experience, I'll ask you once. What do you need?"

That was simple. "You." The dim lighting in the room boosted Lily's courage to sink to her knees and free Reed's cock into her hands here in public. "Just you," she repeated, the surprised pleasure reflected on his face her reward.

"I'm all yours, Lily. I have been for a long time."

She suspected her feelings had started to take hold the moment he whispered those words of always being there for her at John's memorial. For sure, she'd lost her heart the night she found herself drawn to a stranger who cared enough to soothe her distress in a way she'd never imagined. With a taut grip around the base of his thick erection, she flashed him a grin and lowered her head. Licking the softer, mushroom cap, she swiped the pre-cum already seeping from his slit. Lily gloated at the evidence of his arousal, loving how much he always wanted her, no matter when or where, the same as she did him.

Opening her mouth, she took him deep, could feel his blood pumping through the thick veins against her lips, his low groan music to her ears. She scraped her teeth along his rigid length, and he gripped her head to guide her movements, digging his fingers into her scalp. Loving his control, Lily cupped Reed's heavy sac in her palm and used her teeth and tongue to nip and tease up and down his hard flesh. He quickened with a deep suctioning pull, releasing more fluid to slide down her throat. The low voices, music, and erotic cries following sharp contacts with bare skin fell away, her sole focus remaining on thanking Reed for not giving up on her.

To Lily's frustration, he ended her play as she prepared to swallow his climax. Lifting her head, he pushed the thin straps off her shoulders, the loose camisole falling to bare her breasts. Before she realized his intent, he pulled her up for a quick suckle of each turgid nub then stood and flipped her over his shoulder.

With a swat to her upturned butt, he stated, "Time to take this private."

Reed struggled to contain himself until they reached the one room with a bed at the end of the hall. Lily couldn't have found a better way to express herself than opening up like that in front of others, most whom she didn't know. With his heart as ready to burst as his cock, he left the door open and dropped her on the bed. She grinned with an eagerness that matched his, pushing the sexy shorts off as he yanked his jeans down and then lowered himself on top of her. Palming her skull, his fingers tunneled in her hair, he brought them nose-to-nose, lips-to-lips, and asked, "Was that your way of saying yes to a commitment, Lily?"

Without hesitation, her lips brushed his with her reply. "Definitely."

The End

About BJ Wane

I live in the Midwest with my husband and our Goldendoodle. I love dogs, enjoy spending time with my daughter, grandchildren, reading and working puzzles.

We have traveled extensively throughout the states, Canada and just once overseas, but I now much prefer being homebody.

I worked for a while writing articles for a local magazine but soon found my interest in writing for myself peaking.

My first book was strictly spanking erotica, but I slowly evolved to writing steamy romance with a touch of suspense. My favorite genre to read is suspense.

I love hearing from readers. Feel free to contact me at bjwane@cox.net with questions or comments.

Contact BJ Wane

My Website
www.bjwaneauthor.com

My E-mail
bjwane@cox.net

Facebook
www.www.facebook.com/bj.wane
www.facebook.com/BJWaneAuthor

Twitter
www.twitter.com/bj_wane

Instagram
www.instagram.com/bjwaneauthor

Goodreads
www.bit.ly/2S6Yg9F

Bookbub
www.bookbub.com/profile/bj-wane

More Books by BJ Wane

VIRGINIA BLUEBLOODS SERIES
Blindsided
Bind Me to You
Surrender to Me
Blackmailed
Bound by Two

MURDER ON MAGNOLIA ISLAND TRILOGY
Logan
Hunter
Ryder

MIAMI MASTERS SERIES
Bound and Saved
Master Me, Please
Mastering Her Fear
Bound to Submit
His to Master and Own
Theirs To Master

COWBOY DOMS SERIES
Submitting to the Rancher
Submitting to the Sheriff
Submitting to the Cowboy
Submitting to the Lawyer
Submitting to Two Doms
Submitting to the Cattleman
Submitting to the Doctor

COWBOY WOLF SERIES
Gavin (Book 1)
Cody (Book 2)
Drake (Book 3)

DOMS OF MOUNTAIN BEND
Protector (Book 1)
Avenger (Book 2)
Defender (Book 3)
Rescuer (Book 4)
Possessor (Book 5)
Redeemer (Book 6)
Vindicator (Book 7)

THE KINCAID SERIES
Resisting Allie (Book 1)

SINGLE TITLES

Claiming Mia

Masters of the Castle: Witness Protection Program

Dangerous Interference

Returning to Her Master

Her Master at Last

Printed in Great Britain
by Amazon